PONY CLUB
SECRETS

❧Mystic❧
and the
Midnight Ride

The Pony Club Secrets series:

Also Available:

PONY CLUB SECRETS

Mystic
and the
Midnight Ride

Stacy Gregg

HarperCollins *Children's Books*

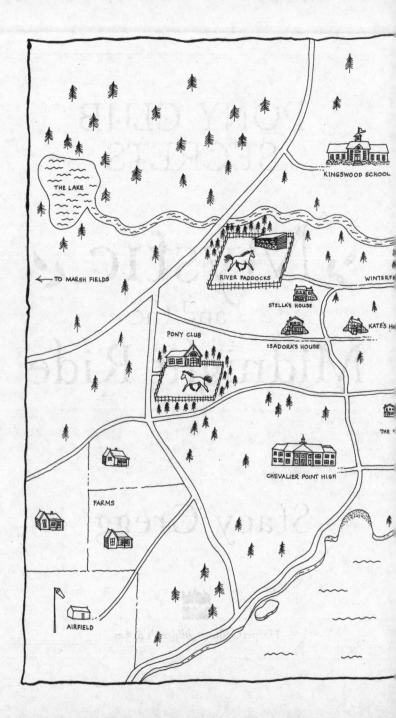

CHEVALIER
POINT

N

FOREST

BEACH

THE POINT

AMON

GOAT ISLAND

For Venetia

www.stacygregg.co.uk

First published in Great Britain by HarperCollins *Children's Books* in 2007.
HarperCollins *Children's Books* is a division of HarperCollins*Publishers* Ltd,
1 London Bridge Street, London SE1 9GF
This edition published in 2014.

www.harpercollins.co.uk

Text copyright © Stacy Gregg 2007

ISBN 978-0-00-724519-2

Stacy Gregg asserts the moral right to be identified
as the author of the work.

Printed and bound by CPI Group (UK) Ltd, Croydon CR0 4YY

MIX
Paper from
responsible sources
FSC
www.fsc.org
FSC™ C007454

FSC™ is a non-profit international organisation established to promote
the responsible management of the world's forests. Products carrying the
FSC label are independently certified to assure consumers that they come
from forests that are managed to meet the social, economic and
ecological needs of present and future generations,
and other controlled sources.

Find out more about HarperCollins and the environment at
www.harpercollins.co.uk/green

CHAPTER 1

Please, please let it be sunny tomorrow, Issie had prayed as she went to bed the night before the gymkhana. But when her alarm clock woke her at quarter to six the next morning and she ran to the window there were grey clouds covering the sky. Still, there was no sign of rain and when she listened for a cancellation on the radio nothing was mentioned, so she headed out into the pre-dawn light to prepare Mystic for his big day.

Stella and Kate were already down at the River Paddock. Stella was busily brushing out Coco's tail, while Kate was sectioning out Toby's neatly pulled mane so that she could start plaiting it into tiny knots along the top of his neck.

"You'd better hurry." Stella smiled. "Tom said he'd be here by seven to help us load them into the truck and take them to the show grounds."

Grabbing Mystic's halter out of the tack room, Issie set off across the paddock. The grass was wet with dew and her riding boots were soaked by the time she reached the spot where Mystic was grazing. The pretty dapple-grey was chewing up great chunks of fresh spring growth and barely bothered to raise his head to acknowledge her.

"Here, Mystic," Issie called hopefully, hiding the halter behind her back with one hand and holding her other hand out towards the pony.

She had forgotten to bring a treat to tempt him with, but perhaps she could bluff the gelding into believing she had a piece of carrot or apple in her empty fist.

No such luck. Mystic had spotted the halter. He gave a deep snort of surprise, shaking his mane and trotting off to the other side of the paddock.

"Oh, Mystic, no! Not today!" Issie cried in despair.

Of course these things always happened at the worst possible moment. Like today. Issie was nervous enough about riding at her first gymkhana. Now she was running late – the others were nearly ready to plait up their horses and she hadn't even started grooming. Even at this distance Issie could see that Mystic had got himself into a right state from rolling in the long paddock grass. There were chunks of dirt matted into his silvery mane and his hocks were stained bright green.

"Come on, Mystic," Issie begged. She bent down, picked a handful of grass and offered it hopefully to the little grey pony. Mystic swivelled his ears towards Issie. He took one step forward, then another. Even though he was knee-deep in grass, the small bunch in Issie's hand was too good to resist. Issie walked quietly up to his side and slid the halter rope around his neck. Then she eased the halter over Mystic's nose and quickly buckled it up behind his ears. Success!

"Who's a naughty pony then?" Stella giggled as Issie led Mystic up to the fence and tethered him next to her Coco.

"It's not just Mystic," Kate insisted. "I spent ages

catching Toby this morning. It's this spring grass. It's making them all act like crazy colts!"

"Do you hear that, Mystic? I bet you wish you were a colt again, eh boy?" Issie laughed.

Mystic wasn't a young horse. Issie had known that when she bought him. Back then she been told that the grey gelding was eighteen. But it was hard to tell the age of a horse. Her pony-club instructor Tom Avery reckoned that the little grey might actually be as old as twenty-five which was positively ancient in horse years.

The pony's dapples had faded over the years from the dark steel of a young colt to a soft dove grey. Mystic's back was slightly swayed too, from years of riding. Still, he was a beautiful pony, only fourteen hands high but he held himself so proudly he seemed bigger. His eyes were dark smudges of coal in his pale face, and they had the calm depth of a horse that has lived a little. Mystic certainly knew his way around a showjumping or cross-country course.

Issie sighed as she examined her horse's hindquarters. "Oh, Mystic, why aren't you a nice dark colour like Toby and Coco? Keeping you clean is twice as much work."

"Don't be so sure," Stella said. "You can't see the grass stains on Coco, but check this out." She gave the chubby little brown mare a friendly slap on the rump and a circle of white dust appeared where her hand had been. "See? I've been grooming for hours now and I can't get rid of it."

Coco turned around to see what Stella was up to and gave her a sniff, nuzzling the girl with her velvet-soft nose. "No, Coco. I don't have any carrots," Stella giggled, "but if you win a ribbon today I promise you can have as many carrots as you want." Coco nickered happily. It was a deal.

Stella and Kate were perfectly suited to their horses, Issie thought. Blonde and blue-eyed Kate was as lanky and long-limbed as her rangy bay Thoroughbred, while Stella, with her bunches of red curls and pale complexion dotted with freckles, was small and bubbly – the same personality as her chocolate-coloured mare.

Stella was Issie's best friend. They had been best friends since the first day of primary school when they realised that not only did they both love horses, they also loved to draw. Even now, art classes were still a competition between the two of them – although their third form art teacher was less than impressed that all they ever wanted to draw was horses.

Issie grabbed a rubber band out of her grooming bucket, using it as a hair tie to secure her long, dark hair out of her face while she worked. Then she dipped her hand back into the bucket of brushes again, this time producing a stiff-bristled dandy brush, and got started on Mystic's hocks, furiously scrubbing away at the mud. She gave Mystic's two white hind socks a brisk scrub with a damp brush to remove the last of the marks, then set about bandaging his legs for the trip. It may only be a few minutes down the road, she figured, but Mystic might still injure his legs in the horse truck if they weren't padded for protection.

The Chevalier Point Pony Club grounds were within riding distance of the River Paddock – about half an hour away at a steady trot. But the stretch of road that you had to ride to reach the pony club was treacherous. The club grounds were just off a busy main road, which made them a nightmare to reach on horseback. Most drivers had no idea of the danger they were causing as they raced past at top speed, never bothering to slow down in case they spooked the horses that were confined to the narrow grass verge on the side of the road.

On rally days, Issie usually rode to pony club the long way, using a series of quiet backroads to reach the grounds, avoiding the main road as much as possible. But today, she wouldn't have to worry about the roads at all. Tom Avery was loading their ponies into his horse truck to drive them to the gymkhana so that they would arrive fresh and ready for the big event.

Issie had bandaged Mystic's tail to keep it clean and was about to start with some last-minute mane-pulling when she heard the stern voice of her pony-club instructor booming out across the paddock. "Come on, girls, I thought you'd have them rugged up and ready to go by now."

Issie turned around to see Avery striding towards her, a tall striking figure in crisp white jodhpurs and long black boots. His face was set in a serious expression underneath the mop of thick, curly brown hair. He held a riding crop in one hand, which Issie had never seen him use – except to thwack against the side of his boot when he was making a point. She guessed he carried it mostly to make himself look meaner.

Sometimes Stella would imitate Avery when he wasn't around, whacking her crop against her leg and barking in a commanding tone, "Come on, chaps, get their hocks under them!" Issie and Kate would hoot with laughter at this impersonation, but the fact was that all three girls had enormous respect for their instructor.

Avery had once been a professional eventer – until he took a bad fall at the Badminton Horse Trials which finished his career for good. He didn't talk much about those days, but Issie knew he had competed against the best riders in the world. He had even been on the same team as Blyth Tait and Mark Todd. But since his accident he didn't ride at all.

Now he worked for the International League for the Protection of Horses, rescuing horses and ponies that had been mistreated and abused by vicious owners, and in his spare time he gave lessons to Issie and the other riders at Chevalier Point.

Hardly a glamorous life for him, Issie thought. After all, Chevalier Point wasn't exactly the most exciting place on earth. It was a small town, perched on a peninsula of land. Issie's mum was fond of saying that there were more horses there than people. Which may have been true. Certainly, if you loved horses then Chevalier Point was the best place in the world to live. With its flat green fields and rolling hills it was perfect horse country.

"Let's get them loaded," Avery instructed the girls. "We've got no time to waste."

"Toby looks great in his new rug," Issie said as Kate led him towards the ramp of the truck. The handsome bay wore a blood-red woollen blanket. Coco, too, was dressed up in her show rug made of navy-blue netting.

Wearing his plain old canvas paddock rug, Mystic didn't look anywhere near as grand. "Don't worry, boy, you look good just as you are," Issie reassured him, worried that her pony's feelings would be hurt if the others got all the attention. Mystic seemed happy enough with Issie's praise. There was a definite spring in his step as he walked up the truck ramp, as if he knew he was on his way somewhere exciting.

Toby whinnied a greeting to Mystic as Issie tied the little grey up in the stall next to the big bay Thoroughbred. She gave each horse a hay net to play with for the five-minute trip and knocked on the window that separated the horses from the passenger cab of the truck to let Avery know they were ready to go. The overcast skies had cleared, the sun was out and they were on their way.

CHAPTER 2

Clouds of dust rose up from the truck tyres as Avery turned off the main road and down the gravel drive that led to the Chevalier Point grounds. Ahead of them were the pony-club gates, hemmed by a line of tall magnolia trees. Beyond the magnolias was another paddock gate and then a series of large plane trees ran like a leafy spine down the middle of the three paddocks that made up the club grounds.

On warm summer days riders could loll about in the shade of the plane trees while their horses rested. It wasn't going to get that hot today. After all, this was the first gymkhana of the season. Still, Avery pulled the horse truck up in the first paddock under two of the biggest trees so that they would be shaded from the glare of the sun.

They unloaded the horses and set to work braiding manes, stencilling chequerboard patterns on to rumps and oiling the ponies' hooves.

Issie had never seen so many riders at Chevalier Point before. The gymkhana was open to all riders in the district, and Issie tried to pick out which riders were from the various clubs by the colour of their jerseys and ties. The Chevalier Point club uniform was a navy jersey with a bright red tie and Issie could see two riders dressed in Chevalier Point colours riding towards her from the far field where the showjumps had been set up.

"Hey, dizzy Issie!" the rider at the front called to her as he cantered closer. "About time you got here. Ben and me have already walked the showjumping course."

Dan and Ben were Chevalier Point Pony Club members. Dan had a flea-bitten grey gelding called Kismit, while Ben rode a grumpy Welsh pony called Max.

"Are the jumps very big?" Issie asked nervously.

"Huge!" Dan teased her. "And you've got to ride fast too, if you want to beat the clock. The best time with no faults wins." He was grinning from ear to ear. Dan was a speed demon. He and Kismit would be the ones to beat in the jumping ring today.

No time to walk the course now, Issie decided. It was nearly time for the first event. She would have to check out the jumps with Stella and Kate during the lunch break.

"Hello, Kismit." Issie reached out a hand to pat the slender grey on the nose. "I suppose you've been promised extra carrots for dinner if you go fast today?" She smiled at Dan.

"Hey! I don't need to bribe my own horse to win." Dan grinned back. "Anyway, we're going to fill in our entry forms now. Do you want to come?" he asked.

Issie was about to say yes when she heard her mother calling her name.

"Isadora! Isadora!" Mrs Brown cried out as she strode across the field towards her. Issie groaned. She couldn't stand the way her mother insisted on using her full name. Isadora. It sounded so snobby and girly, not at all the sort of name for a serious horse rider. Sure, Avery called her Isadora sometimes too, but only when he was telling her off during a riding lesson. Apart from that, everyone else, even her teachers at school, called her Issie.

"I've filled in your entry forms," Mrs Brown explained. "Doesn't Mystic look wonderful?" She gave the grey gelding a very nervous pat and held on to the reins, extending her arm so that she was standing as far away from Mystic as possible while Issie did up the girth.

Everyone said that Issie was exactly like her mum. It was true that they were both tall, tanned and lean with long dark hair. But Issie didn't think they were alike at all. How could they be when Issie loved horses so much and her mother didn't even like them?

Issie wished her mum would give riding a try. Maybe if she could experience for herself the thrill of cantering across open fields with the wind in her hair, she'd finally be able to understand why Issie adored riding so much. But her mum was way too scared to even sit on a horse, let alone canter one.

"What's your first event?" Mrs Brown asked, still reluctantly hanging on to Mystic's reins as Issie finished adjusting her stirrups.

"Paced and Mannered. We're due in the ring any minute now," Issie told her. She gave Mystic a stroke on his dark, velvety nose and her mum gave her a leg up.

"Come on, boy," Issie murmured softly, leaning low over Mystic's neck, "let's show them what we can do."

In the ring, several horses were trotting around warming up. Dan and Ben were already there. A girl that Issie didn't recognise rode in on a skewbald with a peppy trot, a young girl on a chubby chestnut mare following behind her. The chestnut pony had a vicious temper. Her ears were lying flat back against her head – a warning to other horses not to get too close.

The prettiest by far in the ring, thought Issie, was a golden palomino with a star on her forehead and high, lively paces. "Wow! Isn't that palomino gorgeous," Stella said, reading Issie's mind as the two riders sat at the edge of the arena checking out the competition. "I wonder who that rider is? I've never seen her here before but she's wearing our club colours…"

The girl on the palomino had golden hair, almost the same colour as her pony, tied back in two severe plaits. She wore a tweed hacking jacket over her club jersey and had a sour expression on her face.

"I know who it must be," Kate said as she rode up beside them. "That's Natasha Tucker. Her family have just moved here. I bet she's joined Chevalier Point Pony Club!"

The three girls were still eyeing up the palomino with envy, when it suddenly spooked at a plastic bag blowing across the ground. The girl with the sour expression jerked back in the saddle, wrenching on the reins and jagging the little pony sharply in the mouth with the bit. Regaining her seat, she raised her riding crop in the air and brought it down hard on the pony's golden flank. "Stand still you brute!" she squealed.

Issie was stunned. "I can't believe she just did that!"

"Don't worry," muttered Stella, "the judge saw it too and she can't believe it either. Paced and Mannered? More like bad manners! There's no way she's going to get a ribbon for that behaviour. And neither will we for that matter if we don't get in the ring pretty quickly. Come on! The event is about to start."

"Trot on!" ordered the judge, a sturdy woman in blue stockings and a matching straw hat, standing in the middle of the arena. The riders obediently trotted around in a circle.

Issie urged Mystic into a trot and tried to look her best. Heels down, hands still, head up, she chanted to herself as she rose up and down to the rhythm of Mystic's trot.

"Canter!" called the judge. Mystic cantered eagerly around the ring, ears pricked forward, tail held high. Unfortunately his canter was a little too keen. As he got closer to the chubby chestnut mare in front of him she flattened her ears and lashed out with her hind legs. Mystic squealed and shied to one side. Issie let the reins slip and had to grab a handful of mane to stay on his back.

"Halt!" commanded the judge. But there was no hope of that right now. Issie snatched the reins back up but it was too late. Everyone else had stopped their horses and Mystic was still doing an ungainly trot around the ring. She sat down heavy in the saddle and finally he came to a halt. Too late, though – the judge had been watching her mistakes.

When the winners were called into the centre of the ring Issie knew she didn't stand a chance. Kate rode out with a grin on her face and a red ribbon tied around Toby's neck. Behind her was the skewbald in second place and a boy on a brown pony came third.

The haughty girl with the palomino hadn't got anywhere either. As the riders left the ring she barged past Issie and Mystic in a huff. "Get your stupid horse out of the way," she snapped. Then she halted the palomino and turned in the saddle to glare at Issie. Her face was so bitter it looked like she'd been sucking lemons. "It's all your fault anyway," she continued. "If your horse hadn't run wild in there and scared Goldrush I would have won this dumb event. You obviously have no idea how to ride. You shouldn't even be here."

Issie opened her mouth to protest her innocence, but it was too late. The sour-faced girl turned the palomino again and set off at a canter, leaving Issie reeling in shock and anger.

"What was that all about?" Stella rode up to join Issie.

"Well, Stella," Issie said sarcastically, "it looks like I just made friends with the new girl."

As Issie reached Avery's truck she was still deep in thought, mulling over all the things she should have said to nasty old Natasha instead of just sitting there with her mouth hanging open. Then she heard Natasha's shrill voice again. This time, thankfully, she wasn't yelling at Issie. She was talking to someone on the other side of the truck where a silver horse float was parked behind a matching silver sports car.

"Mum, I hate this horse," the girl wailed as she slid off the palomino's back and threw the reins to a tall blonde woman wearing black sunglasses.

"Natasha Tucker!" scolded her mother. "Do you know how much money we've spent on that horse?"

"I don't care!" Natasha barked. "She's useless!"

"Sweetie, please just try to ride her for the rest of the day," her mother sighed. "It seems like every horse we buy for you simply isn't good enough. Give Goldrush a chance."

"All right," Natasha muttered. She was staring at

the ground, kicking the dirt with her riding boot as she sulked. "All right then. But I really can't be bothered. I mean, she's a useless horse. And why do I have to ride anyway? Why won't you buy me a snowboard?"

"Natasha," her mother said firmly, "we've already bought you a jet ski and a pair of rollerblades and a mountain bike, and you don't use any of them. Now, you told us you wanted a pony, and we've paid a small fortune for Goldrush, so you can jolly well get out there and ride her."

With a dramatic sigh of resignation Natasha turned away from her mother and mounted the palomino again, giving her a sharp boot in the ribs as they headed back towards the arena.

Issie couldn't believe it. Was Goldrush just another toy that this girl was getting tired of playing with? How could Natasha Tucker not love the beautiful palomino? And was this awful spoilt brat really the newest member of the Chevalier Point Pony Club?

CHAPTER 3

"Forget about Miss Stuck-up Tucker," Stella giggled. The two girls were sitting on a tartan rug that had been thrown down on the grass next to Avery's truck, noshing into the pile of sandwiches that Issie's mum had prepared for their lunch. "Finish up your sandwich and we'll go grab Kate and walk the showjumping course with Tom."

The showjumping course was laid out at the far end of the club grounds. Avery was already there waiting for them.

"The key to a clear round," he advised them as they set out on foot towards the first jump, "is never take any fence for granted. Especially the first one. Many a rider has a refusal at the first jump because they're too busy thinking about what comes next."

The girls followed along as Avery walked between the fences, describing the various obstacles and advising where the ponies should take off and land. Standing beside the third fence, a parallel rail painted in blue and white stripes, Avery measured the jump against his body. The rail was almost as high as his waist. "These fences are a decent size," he said. "You'll need to be thinking at all times. Keep your horse well-rounded with lots of power in the hindquarters. If you allow them to flatten out you'll never make it over these jumps."

Avery charted out the rest of the course, taking slow careful steps and measuring the strides needed between each fence. "When you're riding I expect you to follow exactly in my footsteps," he told Issie as he walked the line between the fences. "Don't be tempted to cut corners," he said. "Better to risk time faults than to have a refusal."

As they headed back to the truck to saddle up, the girls stopped at the judges' tent and collected their competition numbers, which had been written in black felt tip on to fabric squares that they tied on over their jerseys. Issie was number twenty-two, the last to go. An advantage, she decided, since she could watch the other riders and learn from their mistakes.

"Your first showjumping competition, eh? You must be nervous." Dan gave Issie a grin as he rode up to join her at the side of the show ring.

"Nervous?" Issie tried to act cool even though her tummy was churning with butterflies. "No way! Mystic has done this sort of thing a million times before. I'm pretty relaxed," she said airily.

"Still, hadn't you better go over a few practice jumps?" Dan said, teasing her. "Maybe your problem is that you're a little too relaxed."

Dan was so confident, so self-assured. Issie couldn't stand it any longer. She stared up at him with her hands on her hips. "You think you're so cool, don't you, Daniel Halliday? Well how about a little bet? The losing rider has to groom the winner's horse for a week."

As soon as Issie had opened her mouth she regretted it. What was she saying? Dan hadn't meant to be mean or anything. He only teased her because he liked talking to her, she knew that. She also knew that he was a better rider than she was.

Still, she figured, even losing wouldn't be so bad. She was more than happy to groom Kismit – and hang out with Dan.

Dan removed his helmet, pushing back his blond hair with one hand and then reaching that same hand out to her. "I could use a good groom," Dan smirked. "Let's shake on it."

"Number twenty, Natasha Tucker on Goldrush, please enter the arena," the announcer called over the loudspeaker.

With only three competitors to come, the showjumping course had claimed its fair share of victims. In fact, so far there hadn't been a single clear round. Now it was the turn of Chevalier Point's newest rider to try her luck.

Natasha cantered Goldrush into the ring, pointed the pony towards the first fence and gave her a swift slap with her whip. Goldrush gave a surprised snort and leapt forward, rushing the fence and catapulting Natasha back in the saddle. It wasn't the best start, but somehow Natasha managed to hang on and re-settle herself for the second fence, which Goldrush took with a perfect stride.

One by one, the golden pony took each fence after that without a hitch. As they cleared the final fence, a serious oxer, the crowd let out a cheer. The first clear round of the day. With a fast time too – three minutes and five seconds exactly.

Issie couldn't watch Dan as he entered the ring to begin his round. It wasn't that she was too nervous to watch him; she would have loved to. But she had to warm Mystic up over the practice jump and get him worked in so that he would be ready when her turn came. She rode to the far end of the field and cantered him back and forth over the low crossed rails, all the time half-listening to the loud speaker to hear how Dan was doing. It would be dreadful to lose to Dan, she decided, but much, much worse if they both lost to Natasha.

Issie arrived back at the ringside just in time to see Dan clear the final fence. Kismit took the rails cleanly, then gave a high-spirited buck to signal the end of a clear round, nearly unseating Dan as the pair rode between the flags to finish.

"A clear round in two minutes and forty-four seconds for competitor twenty-one, Dan Halliday," the voice over the loudspeaker announced. "That time puts Dan Halliday in the lead. Would the final competitor, number twenty-two Isadora Brown, please enter the ring."

As the last rider to go, Issie thought to herself, at least she knew where she stood. With only two clear rounds before her, all she needed to do was go clear too and she would win a ribbon. But if she wanted to beat Dan's time? Then she would have to ride faster than she had ever done before in her life.

"Let's go, Mystic," she breathed into the little grey's ear as she leant down low over his neck. Then she squeezed her legs around his plump belly and trotted into the ring. As the judges' bell went to signal the start of the round, Mystic tossed his head and Issie pressed him on into a canter. Her nerves disappeared as she kept her mind focused on clearing the first fence. She sat down heavy and urged Mystic on. He leapt it boldly and fought against her hands to get his head.

"Steady boy," Issie cautioned, holding him firmly and looking to the next fence. Again they took it cleanly and Issie's confidence grew with each jump.

They were gaining speed now, until it seemed to Issie as if she were flying. The grey gelding fought against the bit to go faster still and Issie was forced to hang on tight to the reins to keep Mystic under control.

By the time they rounded the corner to face fences six and seven – a double combination – Mystic was in full stride and too strong for her to hold back. Issie found herself on a sharp angle as the headstrong pony rushed the fence and had to put in a last-minute stride to adjust himself. His hind legs went thwack against the top rail of the first jump and Issie could hear the crowd gasp and hold their breath as the pole rocked in its metal socket. Would the rail fall? She couldn't look, she must concentrate on the next fence ahead of her. She tensed, expecting to hear the crash of the rail falling behind her, but instead she heard a cheer rise up from the crowd. The rail hadn't fallen. She was still clear.

Over the next fence and there she was with just one

jump between her and a clear round. As they neared the big oxer she felt butterflies rise in her tummy and tried to calm herself. "Trust your horse, Issie," she commanded herself out loud. She gave Mystic his head and sat deep in the saddle. The dapple-grey took off perfectly and soared over the rails, landing cleanly on the other side. Clear round!

Mystic was flecked with sweat and snorting from his efforts as the pair left the ring. Issie slid to the ground and threw her arms around his neck giving him a hug and inhaling the sweet smell of warm, damp horse sweat. *It must be the best smell in the world!* Issie thought, breathing in deeply.

"Good lad, Mystic. Well done! A clear round!" she murmured to her pony, her face still buried deep in his grey mane.

"Hey, hey," Dan called as he rode over to her, "what are you doing? Get back on your horse – you'll have to ride into the ring in a minute to get your ribbon!"

But which ribbon? With three clear rounds, Issie's time was crucial now. Had she gone fast enough to beat Dan?

"Competitor number twenty-two, Isadora Brown,

a clear round in two minutes fifty-six seconds," the announcer called. "The winner is Dan Halliday on Kismit. Second place goes to Isadora Brown on Mystic, third Natasha Tucker on Goldrush. Would all riders please come back into the ring to collect your prizes."

As Mystic trotted into the arena, Issie felt like she was in a dream. It didn't matter that Dan had beaten her. She had won her first ribbon. Mystic seemed to know it too; as the three riders cantered around the ring in a lap of honour he bristled with pride, flicking his tail and arching his neck.

"You are totally the best pony ever, do you know that?" Issie told Mystic as they rode back to Avery's truck. "Just the best," she repeated again proudly as she pulled the little grey up to a halt. OK, so she'd lost her bet with Dan and she'd have to groom Kismit for a week – she didn't care. Second place. And a clear round! How fantastic was that?

Issie was just about to dismount and give Mystic yet another hug when she heard someone crashing about on the other side of the silver horse float.

"Stop that! Stand still, damn you!" Natasha Tucker's voice was raised in a high-pitched squeal. She had been trying to take off Goldrush's tack but the pretty palomino kept dancing nervously as the girl tried to undo her bridle. "Stop it!" Natasha shouted again, this time giving Goldrush a slap across the neck with her riding crop.

As the whip cut hard into her flesh the palomino reared up, jerking the reins out of Natasha's hands. Natasha stood there helplessly as Goldrush planted her front legs back on the ground, standing on top of the loose reins and tangling them around her legs.

Caught in the reins, Goldrush went wild with terror. The mare tried to back up to get free, but found herself pressed up hard against Toby and Coco who were tied to the truck beside her.

What happened next came so suddenly that Issie didn't have a chance to stop it. She watched as Goldrush kept backing up into the other horses, kicking out in terror with her hind legs. Then Toby gave a snort and pulled back hard against his halter rope. The knot gave way and his lead rope came loose. Coco, too, had worked her way free from her tether. Now, all three horses were loose and heading for the paddock gate.

It was then that Issie noticed that the main pony club gate was still open – someone must have forgotten to shut it as they had driven in to park their horse float.

"Hey! The gates. Shut the gates!" Issie yelled.

As the horses bolted through the first paddock gate and headed for the main gate, Issie saw people running after them, trying to divert them from the exit. *It's no use,* she realised. *They'll never catch up with them on foot.* But maybe she could reach them on Mystic.

She wheeled the little grey around and clucked him into a canter, leaning low over his neck. The horses were through the gate now and already clattering along the gravel driveway that would lead them to the deadly road.

In full gallop now, Issie and Mystic rounded through the gate behind them. "Come on, boy, we've got to beat them to the road." Issie dug her heels into Mystic's sides, urging him on even faster. Mystic was gaining on the horses but as they got closer to the intersection where the roads met, Issie realised they weren't going to make it in time. She would have to ride out on to the road after the horses and try to herd them back again.

The clatter of gravel became the clean chime of metal horseshoes hitting tarmac as the horses struck the main highway. There was the honk of a car horn as two vehicles sped past, one of them narrowly missing Toby.

Issie quickly checked for more traffic then followed the runaway horses out on to the road. She pulled Mystic around hard in front of Toby and waved an arm at him, spooking the big bay and directing him back down the gravel drive, back towards the pony club.

If she could get Toby to lead the way, maybe the others would follow. It was their only chance. Two cars had already nearly hit them. How long could their luck last?

Suddenly the deep low boom of a truck horn sounded off behind her. Issie heard the sickening squeal of tyres and smelt burning rubber. As the truck rounded the corner towards her, everything suddenly seemed to go into slow motion.

To Issie it seemed as if Mystic was turning to face the truck, like two stallions set to fight. The grey horse reared up suddenly, throwing her backwards with such force that she flew clear of the oncoming traffic, landing hard on the shoulder of the road. There was a sickening crack as her riding helmet met with tarmac, the peak splintering as it took the full force of the blow.

Groggy from the fall, Issie tried to stand up, to move, but her vision blurred and she could taste blood in her mouth. In the distance came the screech of tyres again and then the most hideous sound she had ever heard, the sound of a horse screaming. Through the sirens and the traffic noise she could make out a voice calling out her name, and then everything faded to black.

CHAPTER 4

Issie could hear hoofbeats. In the pitch black she saw the blurry grey shape of a horse galloping towards her. Just out of her reach, the horse reared to a stop. His nostrils flared, and he pawed the ground impatiently, flicking his head and nickering to her. Then, as suddenly as he had come, he wheeled around and galloped away again. Mystic? It had to be. Issie tried to yell out to him but she couldn't speak. What was happening to her?

"I think she's coming round," a voice broke through the blackness.

Then another voice, softer, calling her, "Isadora. Isadora. Wake up."

And there she was, lying between the cool white sheets of a hospital bed, looking up into her mother's eyes.

"My God, Isadora! You gave me such a scare." Mrs Brown had tears in her eyes as she hugged her daughter tightly. The embrace was so strong, Issie found it hard to breathe and had to gasp for air. As she took a deep breath her chest ached and she let out a squeal of pain.

"Do your ribs hurt?" A woman in a white coat was leaning over her. Issie nodded yes.

"Isadora, my name is Doctor Stone," the woman said. "I don't think your ribs are broken. I suspect it's just bruising. We'll be sending you down to x-ray shortly to check. But first I need to ask you a few questions, just to check that you're OK. You had a bad fall and you may be suffering from concussion." The doctor held up her hand. "How many fingers am I holding up?"

"Three," said Issie. She was surprised at how wobbly her voice was. "And what day is it?" Doctor Stone asked as she checked Issie's eyes with a little torch light. "Umm… Saturday?"

"Excellent." The doctor was making notes on her

chart now as she talked. "How old are you, Isadora?"

"Twelve," Issie had to think for a moment, "but I'll be thirteen soon."

Doctor Stone gave her young patient a concerned look. "Now, I want you to think carefully, Isadora. I want you to try to remember the last thing that happened to you. Do you know why you're here?"

Issie shut her eyes and tried to think. What had happened to her? She remembered the sound of a truck horn, and the way Mystic had reared up, as if to protect her from the huge steel vehicle that was bearing down on them. Then nothing, nothing but the tarmac rushing up to meet her, that inhuman scream and then the blackness.

"Where is Mystic?" Issie felt a wave of panic sweep over her. "Mum, is Mystic OK?"

Her chest ached sharply as she tried to sit up. "Isadora, please try and stay still until we can get those ribs x-rayed," Doctor Stone said firmly. She turned to Mrs Brown. "I don't think we'll need to keep her in overnight. If the x-ray comes out OK, she can be discharged this evening."

"But what about my horse?" Issie was cold with

horror as she spoke. Her mum kept ignoring her questions about Mystic. Something was wrong. Mrs Brown had turned her head away from her now. At first she couldn't speak. Finally, she faced her daughter and took her hand. Her words came softly but in Issie's ears they were like crashes of thunder.

"Isadora, there was nothing anyone could have done. The truck…" Her mother's voice trailed off for a moment. "…Isadora, Mystic is dead."

"No!" Issie felt hot tears running down her cheeks. She was shaking, gasping once more for breath. "No!"

"I'm sorry, honey." Her mother was still clutching her hand, and she was crying too. "Stella saw it all from the side of the road. You and Mystic saved the other horses, you know. If you hadn't gone after them and herded them back up the driveway, who knows what would have happened. But then the truck came…" Mrs Brown stroked away her daughter's tears. "You know, I think Mystic was trying to save you too. When he reared up and threw you clear of the truck, it saved your life. So it wasn't just the other horses he saved. He saved you."

"Isadora," the doctor interrupted, "I'm just going

to give you a sedative. It'll take away the pain and let you relax for a while."

Issie nodded vacantly. She didn't really hear what the doctor was saying, and she could no longer feel the pain in her ribs. Instead, it was her heart that ached. An ache that consumed her entire soul. Mystic was dead.

Issie barely even noticed the sting of the injection that Doctor Stone gave her, but she began to feel its effects almost immediately. She felt woozy, and her muscles went limp. Through half-closed eyes she could see her mother sitting beside the bed holding her hand, then she drifted off, back into darkness, back into black sleep.

Her mother was still sitting by the bed two hours later when she opened her eyes again.

"How are you feeling, honey?" Mrs Brown ran her hand softly over her daughter's forehead, smoothing back her dark hair. Issie's complexion, usually a light olive colour just like her mum's, was so drained and pale she was almost the same colour as the hospital sheets.

"I've telephoned your dad," Mrs Brown told her, still stroking her hair as she spoke. "He said he would fly up to see you, but I told him it would be OK, that you were likely to be going home tonight. Still, he was very worried about you."

"Sure he was," Issie said. Since her mum and dad divorced three years ago it seemed like she hardly even existed. Her father had remarried and had a whole new family in another city now and it had been months since she saw him last. What made her mum think that just because she'd been in an accident he would come running?

"Anyway, he sent you these." Mrs Brown lifted up a pot of yellow chrysanthemums and plonked them down on the table by Issie's bed.

"Issie," Mrs Brown took her daughter's hand, "when you're ready to talk about what happened to Mystic..."

"Mum, I don't want to. Not yet…" Issie was trying hard not to start crying all over again. She looked down at the bed clothes, refusing to meet her mother's eyes. "Can't I... can't we just go home now? I just want it all to be over."

"I'm sorry, I hope I'm not interrupting?" Doctor Stone entered the room. "Only we really need to get Isadora down to x-ray now."

Mrs Brown sighed. "Of course. We can talk later when we get home."

Two hours later, the x-rays had been taken and Doctor Stone's diagnosis was confirmed: no broken bones, just some bruising, slight concussion and a large swollen lump at the front of her head where the peak of the helmet had connected with the road.

Issie was getting dressed to go home when she heard a knock. "Can we come in?" Stella and Kate stuck their heads around the corner of the door to Issie's room. Issie gave them a weak smile and the two girls entered the room and sat down beside her bed. Kate looked pale with shock and Stella's freckled face was flushed hot pink from crying.

"How are Toby and Coco?" Issie wanted to know.

"Well, Toby has gone lame. But it's nothing serious. The vet thinks it's a stone bruise from galloping on the gravel but he should be OK in a week or so." Kate managed a grin.

"And Coco is just fine. She threw a shoe, but she wasn't hurt," Stella continued. "In fact, that run is probably the most exercise she's had in years!"

"If you and Mystic hadn't caught up with them…" Stella sighed. "Well, it was just the bravest thing I've ever seen." She looked down at her shoes for a moment and then back at Issie. "I mean, I know there's nothing I can do to bring Mystic back, but Kate and I were thinking… if you wanted to, you could ride Coco and Toby any time you like. We could even work out a roster. You could have Coco on Mondays and Tuesdays and ride Toby on Wednesdays…" She paused as Issie began to cry.

"Oh, Issie, I know it's not the same as having your own horse but…"

Issie shook her head. "It's not that. Don't you see? I don't want another horse. Not after what happened to Mystic. I couldn't… I'm never going to ride again."

That night, home from the hospital, Issie found it hard to sleep. When she did finally close her eyes, the vision of the grey ghost horse returned. There was the pounding of hooves, and then once again the horse appeared and reared to a halt just out of Issie's reach.

This time she could see his face more clearly. The smouldering charcoal eyes, the velvety nostrils flared with tension. It was Mystic. She was sure of that now. She held out her hand and the horse whinnied gently, lowering his head so that the tip of his nose traced just above the ground as he stepped towards her. Issie knew that the lowered head was part of "horse language". It was Mystic's way of saying, "I know you. I trust you. You're part of my herd."

She spoke softly to him now, "Easy, Mystic, easy, boy. It's me, boy..." Her hand reached out and Issie felt a shock of wonder as her fingers touched the silver tussock of his mane. The sensation of the coarse, ropey hair against her skin was totally real. This horse was no ghost! It was as alive as she was. Why, if she only reached out her other hand and grabbed on to his mane, she was sure she could swing herself up on to Mystic's back and ride him. Ride him just as she had done before the accident had ruined everything. She reached out a hand, but Mystic stepped backwards and pawed fitfully at the ground with his left front hoof. Then he turned again and galloped off, the silver stream of his tail disappearing into the blackness.

"I know it sounds stupid," Issie told her mum at breakfast the next day, "but it was as if he was real. I mean, I know it must have been a dream, but it didn't feel like a dream. It was like Mystic was really there, right in front of me. I even touched him!"

"Oh, sweetheart," Mrs Brown took her daughter's small, tanned hand in her own, "you had a bad fall and you've been through a terrible experience. It's only natural that you'll be pretty shaken up for a while. But you have to face up to what has happened. I know it hurts and you miss Mystic. But you're lucky to be alive."

Mrs Brown smiled gently as she reached over and poured out a cup of hot chocolate for Issie and a fresh cup of tea for herself. "Your father and I have discussed the best thing to do about this…" Mrs Brown looked down at her cup of tea. She paused, unable to get the words out. "Isadora, I know how much you love horses. And I know what happened wasn't your fault. You were very brave to do what you did. But, well, your father agreed with me on this…" Mrs Brown finally looked her daughter in the face.

"Issie, I can't let you have another horse. It was so terrifying when you were in that hospital bed and I didn't know whether you would even wake up. I couldn't go through that again. I am your mother and… oh, Issie, you have to understand I can't risk something else happening to you. I know that you want to get another horse and—"

"No, Mum, you don't understand!" Issie felt hot tears well in her eyes. How could her mum even think she would want a new horse? All she wanted was Mystic. She wanted her horse to come back to her. How could she explain to her mother that Mystic was more than just some pony to her? That he had been her closest friend, the one soul that she could confide all her secrets to, because he would never betray her. A kindred spirit who she could trust totally and love absolutely. The most important thing in her life. The truth was, she couldn't explain it to her mother, or to anyone.

Issie took a deep breath and kept her eyes on the bowl of cereal in front of her. "I don't care anyway." Issie could feel the tears running down her cheeks; she wanted to stop crying but she couldn't. She wiped her cheeks roughly with her sleeve and faced her mother. "I said that I was never going to ride again, and I meant it."

CHAPTER 5

"You know Lisa Jones?" Stella was chattering away and looking absent-mindedly for a book in her school bag as they walked into Mrs Carter's classroom for fourth period maths. "Well," Stella continued, "her family moved to the Hawkes Bay and she had to go to this new school. I think it's called Iona College. Anyway, it's very posh and they get to ride horses at school. Can you believe it? Horse riding is actually a school subject! So instead of doing a stinky old maths class, you could go riding instead. Lisa grazes her horse there and she's allowed to go and check on him at lunchtimes, and they even have proper stables with loose boxes to keep them in. I mean, that would be so cool, wouldn't it?"

Issie just nodded, and headed for the back of the classroom, taking her usual seat at the far corner of the room. She was sick and tired of hearing stories about horses and how much fun they were. It seemed like ever since she told Stella and Kate that she wasn't going to ride any more, the pair of them had been trying to come up with new ways to get her interested in riding again. OK, she knew her friends were just trying to help, but she wished they would leave her alone.

Stella leaned over from her desk and whispered to Issie, "Hey, Kate and I were thinking that after school, if you're not busy—"

Issie groaned and cut her off in mid-sentence, "Stella, I don't want to go riding. Not this afternoon. Not ever!"

"OK, OK, get over yourself," Stella sneered back. "What I was going to say is that me and Kate, well, you know how Kallista Field has a pierced belly button? Well, they do piercings at Lacey's chemist shop and we were thinking of getting them done too."

Of course Issie knew all about Kallista Field. There were always stories about the young dressage rider in

PONY Magazine. Issie even had pictures of Kallista up on the wall in her bedroom. Kallista wasn't just a good rider, she was also tall and beautiful with long blonde hair. And she had a pierced belly button. Issie had seen it in photos and she had to admit, it did look pretty cool.

Stella kept on talking, "Kate says she still can't decide whether to get one or not. But we were talking to Louisa Bull – she's really cool, she's a fourth former but I know her because she's in my house – anyway, she has one and it looks so fab and she says it didn't hurt much at all." She poked Issie in the tummy and grinned. "You would look so good with one, Issie. So what do you say? Are you in?"

Issie winced and pulled up her jersey to look at her naked belly button. It was an innie, not an outie, a small, delicate whirl in the middle of her olive-skinned tummy. She imagined the piercing gun clamped over it, driving a steel ring through her skin.

"I don't know…" Issie muttered. "Mum wouldn't be too keen on it…"

"It's OK," Stella insisted. "I asked Penny and she said she would take us, so you don't need to ask your mum."

Penny was Stella's older sister. She was much older than Stella and was in her first year at university. The two sisters both had the same curly red hair and freckles – and the same naughty streak too. If anything, Penny was even wilder than her little sister. And Stella always wanted to do what Penny did. Penny already had her belly button pierced – and her tongue!

"Come on," Stella was whining. "Your mum won't even notice. We'll all do it together. It'll be fun."

Issie took her hand off her stomach and tucked the thin cotton of her school shirt back into her skirt, smoothing it down flat. She had always wanted to get a piercing. Even plain pierced ears weren't allowed at Chevalier Point High. But a belly button? Who would ever notice it underneath your school uniform?

OK, so her mum would kill her if she found out. But who cared? Besides, why shouldn't she have some fun and do something exciting for once? She was so tired of feeling this way, tired of being numb and depressed. Maybe Stella was right. It would look pretty cool to have a belly-button ring like Kallista.

"What sort of rings are there?" Issie sighed.

Stella let out a squeal of delight. "Yay! I knew you'd

say yes! This is going to be great! There's plain silver ones, or you can get ones with a stone in them," Stella continued. "I was thinking of getting maybe a purple stone like an amethyst but you can get whatever you want." She looked at Issie's screwed-up face. "I swear. Honestly. It doesn't hurt!"

A couple of hours later, Issie wished she had never taken Stella's word for it. There she was, lying flat on her back on the thin white chemist shop bunk bed, looking down at her skin stretched taut under the clamp of the piercing gun. There was a felt-tip dot on her belly button where the ring would pierce the skin, and a woman with too much make-up on was busily daubing her tummy with antiseptic solution.

"Now take a deep breath and breathe out as the needle goes through," the woman instructed. Issie looked away from the gun, trying not to think about it as she sucked in a deep lung full of air. As she breathed out she felt a sudden rush of pain.

"There. You're done." The woman smiled. Issie

looked down at her newly decorated navel. It was red and tingling. "You'll have to keep it very clean for the first couple of weeks while it heals, and whatever you do, don't take the ring out," the woman instructed, passing Issie some antiseptic to take home with her. "And try not to wear clothes that rub on it and irritate the site."

"I can't believe you two went through with it!" Kate shrieked as the three girls came out of the chemist into the bright sunlight to meet her.

"What? I can't believe you chickened out on us!" Stella teased her back.

"I didn't!" Kate insisted. "I never said I would get one. I only said I was thinking about it." She leaned down and peered closer at Issie's red, swollen belly button and pulled a face. "Eugh! Does it hurt?"

Issie looked pleased with Kate's reaction. "Not really," she lied. In fact, she could feel her tummy button all hot and throbbing where the ring had gone through.

"You know," Stella began, "when Louisa Bull had hers done she told me that it went all infected and she woke up one morning and, oh, this is really going to gross you out, her mum had to take her to hospital because—"

"Stella! I thought you told me that Louisa's belly button looked really cool?" Issie yelped. "What happened?"

"Nothing happened!" Penny snapped. "Stella! She didn't go to hospital, she just went to the doctor and he gave her some ointment to put on it and sent her home again. Stop exaggerating and making up horrible stories."

Penny pulled up her own t-shirt to show them her belly button. It had a silver ring with a green glass leaf dangling down from it. "Look, I've had my piercing for two years now and it's fine," she reassured Issie.

"I was just joking!" Stella insisted, grinning mischievously. "Hey, Issie, let's go back to your house and try on clothes. I need to find a tank top that will show off my tummy button."

The Browns had lived in the same house ever since Issie was little. It was a two-storey wooden home, surrounded by rambling, overgrown gardens. From Issie's bedroom upstairs she had a view down over the big back lawn to the grove of trees at the end of the garden.

The view inside Issie's bedroom, however, was one big mess. The girls had spent the past hour trying on everything in Issie's wardrobe and the place looked like a stall at a jumble sale. There were pairs of jeans and shoes thrown all over the floor, and the bed was stacked so high with piles of clothes that you could barely see Stella and Kate, who were flopped down in the middle of it all on top of the duvet.

Issie stepped out of the wardrobe. She had stripped off the light-green pleated skirt and white shirt of her school uniform and was wearing a purple floral crop top and dark blue camouflage pants. She stood in front of the mirror to admire her new look. For once, her skinny boyish figure was working to her advantage. The pants hung down so low on her hips they exposed her stomach, showing off the freshly pierced navel.

Issie stared at her tummy button. It was still swollen and red, and even though she would never admit it, she was a little worried about what she had done. Stella's story had scared her. What if the piercing really was turning septic? The skin around the ring did actually look all red and raw and it was hurting a lot more than she had thought it would.

Issie shrugged off her fears. At least Stella had been right about one thing, she thought, that silver ring did look pretty cool. It suited her, the slim metal circle resting perfectly against her tanned belly.

Issie was wiggling the ring and gazing at her reflection when she suddenly noticed the other two girls staring at her. Feeling embarrassed to suddenly be the centre of attention, she struck a ridiculous supermodel catwalk pose, pouting and throwing her head back, one hand on her hip, the other raised to blow a kiss to an imaginary camera.

The two girls fell about on the bed laughing. Stella was snorting so hard she was almost choking and Issie collapsed on to the duvet next to her in a fit of giggles.

As she lay there panting with laughter she realised this was the first time since the accident that she had been able to forget about Mystic and have some fun.

"Wait, wait!" Stella leapt up and grabbed a pair of sunglasses off the dressing table. She put them on, along with a pair of foolishly high heels that Issie had borrowed out of her mum's room, and began strutting up and down the bedroom. "Who am I?" she asked giggling. "I'll give you a clue," she added, clearing her throat and talking in a mock posh voice. "I want a new pony! I want to go snowboarding! I'm a spoilt brat!"

"Oh, don't…" Issie tried to stop laughing so that she could get the words out. "…we shouldn't make fun of Natasha. It's mean."

"That's easy for you to say!" Stella snapped. "You haven't had to put up with her at pony-club rallies for the past month. Honestly, she is such a snob she won't even speak to Kate and me! At lunchtimes she ties her horse up at the other end of the paddock and refuses to even come near us."

Stella looked distracted for a moment, then she bent over and examined her stomach. "I hope this ring doesn't get caught on my jodhpurs when I'm riding." She frowned.

Then she noticed Issie throwing her a sulky look.

"Oops. Sorry, Issie. I keep forgetting that you don't want to talk about horses." Stella smiled. "I guess I just can't believe it, really. I know you feel awful about what happened to Mystic. But it was an accident. And, well, I don't mean to be harsh, but Mystic was really old. So at least he didn't have much longer to live anyway."

Issie couldn't believe what she was hearing. She was used to her friend's lack of tact. Stella had a habit of saying the wrong thing at the wrong time. But this was a bit much even from her. How would she feel if it was Coco that had died? Issie was trying so hard to hold back the tears that she felt too choked up to say anything. She wanted to say that Mystic was special. That he was her horse and that he may have been old but he had a young spirit that refused to give up. She wanted to tell her two friends how she still saw him every night. A silver ghost horse, too real to be just a dream. So real he felt like flesh and blood. Somehow Mystic was still there with her. She just wished she knew why.

The phone in the hallway rang. "I'll get it," Issie squawked, keen to escape this dreadful conversation, and the horrible feeling of tears welling up yet again in her eyes. She ran down the corridor, sliding on the hall rug as she made a grab for the receiver. It was Tom Avery's voice on the other end of the line.

"I've been trying to get in touch with you since this morning." Avery sounded serious. "Listen, Issie, something has come up. Can you meet me down at the horse paddock tomorrow morning at around eight?" He paused. "And bring the key to the tack room with you."

When Issie asked him why, Avery became even more mysterious. "I need you to help me with something, that's all," he said, hanging up before she had a chance to ask any more questions.

Before Issie went to bed that night she set her alarm clock and laid out her favourite old faded blue jeans and a pair of boots to wear the next morning. She hadn't spoken to Avery at all since the accident. And now this. Why was he being so mysterious? And what did he need her help for?

She sat down on the bed and pulled up her pyjama top to have one last look at her newly pierced belly button before she went to sleep. "Oh, well," she muttered to herself, wiggling the little silver ring with her index finger, "nothing could surprise me now."

But she was wrong.

CHAPTER 6

The pony-club paddocks were deserted when Issie arrived, except for the horses dotted about the field, grazing in the morning sun. Avery was nowhere to be seen, so Issie climbed over the fence and unlocked the tack room.

Standing in the tack room, she felt a rush of emotion as she looked at the hook and saddle horse where she had kept Mystic's things. His leather halter and canvas paddock cover were still hanging there, but the saddle horse was bare. When Mystic had gone under the truck, her beloved Stübben saddle had been destroyed too. Not that it mattered, Issie reminded herself. She didn't need a saddle because she wasn't going to ride ever again.

As a further reminder of her vow, up there on the wall next to the empty saddle rack was a photograph. It was her and Mystic; taken the day that she had first brought the dapple-grey here to his new home. It must have been the end of winter, because Mystic's coat was thick and fluffy with winter growth. His mane was long and flowing; it obviously hadn't been pulled in months. His eyes were dark and steady, staring straight at the camera. And there she was with him, the wind whipping her long dark hair across her face so that her eyes were barely visible. She had one hand on Mystic's wither and the other holding his lead rope. They made the perfect team.

"There you are!" Avery's voice behind her made her jump. "Come on out for a moment, I've got something to show you. Oh, and bring that halter. You're going to need it."

Issie emerged into the sunlight to see Avery's horse truck parked outside the gate. He climbed back into the cab again and gestured for her to swing the gate open to let him drive through.

As Issie closed the gate behind him, she watched Avery ease the vehicle alongside the loading ramp. When he pulled the truck to a stop, she could hear the uncertain shift of hooves against the matting floor. There was a horse in there! Of course! Why else would Avery tell her to bring a halter with her. But which horse? She looked out across the paddock to see Toby and Coco both grazing peacefully at the far end of the field. It wasn't them on the truck then, but... The stamp of hooves became more restless and the high-pitched nicker of a horse could clearly be heard from inside the truck.

Avery leapt down from the driver's seat and strode over to her. "Good, good," he said. "All set then? Let's go!" He began to unbolt the doors. "Issie you go in and put her halter on. We'll put her in the pen by the tack room for the time being."

"What? What are you talking about?" Issie didn't understand.

"Oh, right. I'm sorry." Avery smiled. "It's a horse, Issie. And I want you to have her." He held up his hand to stop her cries of protest. "Look, I didn't mean to spring it on you like this. I understand how much it hurt you to lose Mystic. And maybe it is a little soon to expect you to get back into the saddle again. But I had no choice. You know about my work with the International League for the Protection of Horses, don't you?"

Issie nodded.

"It's my job to investigate reports of horses that are being mistreated or badly looked after by their owners. And if those horses are being neglected, then it's also my job to take them away and find new homes for them. People can be unbelievably cruel," Avery continued, shaking his head, unable to disguise the disgust in his voice. "Can you even imagine, Issie? No grass to eat, just dirt to live on. A paddock no bigger than a cattle pen. When the horse protection league found this mare, she was… well, you'll see for yourself in just a moment what sort of a state she is in.

"Issie, I know it's not fair to ask this from you. This mare is in a delicate condition. She's very sick, one of the worst cases I've ever seen." Avery's face was grim. "She needs round the clock care from someone who really understands horses if she's going to pull through. Even then she may not survive… And I know you're still hurting from losing Mystic. But when I saw her I knew that you were the one to take care of her. To love her. Because she'll need someone like you, someone who truly loves horses, who has a way with them, to bring her back to life."

A faint, nervous whinny came from behind the door. "Now, come on," Avery looked at her intently, "what do you say?"

Issie knew that there was nothing she could say. She just nodded to Tom, and stepped to the side so that he could open the door and let her in.

In her worst nightmares, Issie had never seen anything like the sight that was now before her. In the centre stall of the truck stood a chestnut mare. At least Issie supposed she was a chestnut. The pony's coat was so covered in mud, and worn thin in great patches, that you could hardly tell what colour she was at all. From beneath the caked mud, her ribs stuck out sharply through her skin. Her rump, rather than being rounded and firm, was hollowed out where the muscles should have been. And the pony's legs were covered in mud sores. But it was the pony's expression which upset Issie most of all. The little mare wouldn't even raise her head to look at Issie, and when she finally did look her way, her eyes showed pure terror. As Issie got closer the mare let out a long, low snort of fear. But she didn't attempt to back away. It was as if her spirit was so broken she didn't care what happened to her any more.

"Easy now, girl," Issie cooed as she put the halter on. The chestnut mare flinched away from her hands as Issie fastened the halter buckle, but she was too weak to put up much of a fight. "Easy now," she murmured again, stroking the length of the mare's slender neck. Underneath the dry mud on her legs Issie could make out four white socks, and down the mare's dainty face ran a white blaze.

"What's her name?" Issie asked Avery as she tried to cluck the mare into moving forward and out of the truck stall.

"Doesn't have one, I'm afraid," Avery said. "At least, we don't think she has a name. We never did track down the people who did this to her. We're trying to trace the owners so that animal cruelty charges can be laid against them, but it's not easy. So… no owners and no name."

"I think we should call you Blaze," Issie whispered to the mare, "after that pretty white blaze that's running down the middle of your face."

"Hey, hey, wait a minute," Avery smirked, "you can't just go ahead and name this horse." He paused. "Unless, that is, unless you're willing to keep her?"

"Oh, Tom," Issie sighed, "of course I'll keep her. Like you said, I don't have a choice, do I?"

"You understand the rules of the ILPH, don't you?" Avery asked. "If a horse comes into our care we can appoint a guardian for that horse. But that's all you will ever be to Blaze – her guardian. You don't own her, so she's not yours to sell. If you ever change your mind about her or can't look after her you must return her to the League and they'll find a new home for her."

Issie nodded, then turned to the chestnut mare. "Do you hear that, girl? I'm your new guardian. And I'm going to take real good care of you. Come on now, come out and see your new home."

Issie led Blaze down the truck ramp and her heart nearly broke as she watched the little mare, all wobbly on her feet, gingerly putting one hoof in front of another.

She tied the chestnut to a fence rail. It had been hard to really examine her in the truck. Now, in the bright sunlight, she stood back and took a long hard look. She was definitely a pony, not a horse; Issie guessed she stood somewhere between fourteen and fourteen-two hands high. And there was no doubt that she was well bred. Even in such pitiful condition the mare showed signs of her Arab bloodlines. The classic dished nose and finely pricked ears gave her away. As did her legs, slender and delicate like a ballet dancer's.

In the sunlight the mare's coat was darker than Issie had first thought, a deep liver chestnut. Her mane and tail were a light shade of honey, almost flaxen blonde. Looking down at her legs, Issie could see that she did indeed have four white socks. In fact, the two hind socks were almost stockings – running all the way right up to her hocks, while the white blaze which began as a large star on her forehead continued in a slender streak all the way down her face to her velvety nostrils where it finally tapered away.

"She's beautiful, Tom," Issie breathed softly.

"We'll have to keep her in the pen for a couple of days or so, I'm afraid," Avery said briskly. "She's too weak to be let loose to graze with the other horses at this stage. If they took to her she'd never survive the fight. I'll try and sort out the grazing so she can have a paddock to herself in a day or two and in the meantime you'll have to start bulking her up on hard feed and hay."

Avery looked concerned. "We're talking about more than a physical problem with this mare though, Issie. It's her mind that needs the most care. She's been through a lot. Whoever owned her must have abused her terribly. She doesn't know how to trust people any more. And it's going to take a lot of work and patience to win back that trust.

"Might as well get to work on the physical stuff straight away though, eh?" Avery pointed to Issie's grooming kit and gave her a knowing grin. "I'll bet there's a decent coat under all that mud, so get to it! I've got to dash. You need to spend some time, to know her better. And," Avery added, "of course you'll need to talk to your mum about things too – but I'm sure she'll be fine about it, won't she?"

Issie was about to respond to this and point out that, actually, her mum wouldn't be fine about it at all. But Avery wasn't listening.

"Excellent then! Right. I'm off. I'll check up on you both next week."

And with that, Avery backed the truck out of the gate and left Issie standing there open-mouthed.

Issie stood there for a moment longer, watching the truck as it became smaller in the distance. Then she turned back to the horse and reached for her bucket of grooming brushes. As she lifted the dandy brush towards Blaze to scuff off the dried mud, the pony let out a terrified snort and pulled back hard against the rope, her eyes wild with fear.

"Easy, girl, I'm not going to hurt you," Issie murmured. She put the brush down and reached her hand up to stroke Blaze's neck and calm her down. But the mare wasn't having any of it. She backed up, straining against the rope, her ears flat back against her head.

Issie felt terrible. She knew Blaze wasn't acting up on purpose. It was simply that the poor horse had been so badly abused in the past she was scared of being touched. Issie realised it was only natural that Blaze would be scared of her too, but it still hurt.

Once more she moved slowly towards the horse, and Blaze backed even further away, letting out a low, long snort of terror.

"Blaze! How can I brush you if you won't even let me get near you?" Issie pleaded, close to despair. Then she had an idea. In the tack room there were three large bins of hard feed for the horses, the first two filled with oats and chaff and the third with pony pellets. Issie grabbed a handful of these and walked back over to Blaze.

This time the nervous chestnut didn't back away. She sniffed the air, then stretched out her long, elegant neck as far as she could without actually stepping forward. Food. She could smell it all right. But was she brave enough to take it? Still not moving a single hoof, the mare craned her neck even further, then used her rubbery lips to stretch out and snuffle up the pellets out of Issie's hand.

"Good girl, Blaze," Issie murmured, reaching her

hand out once more to stroke the horse. Blaze let Issie's fingertips graze against her mud-coated neck before she backed up once again, heaving with fear.

"Easy, girl, it's OK," Issie said, backing away herself, admitting defeat. She went back to the tack room a second time, but when she emerged again she wasn't carrying a handful of pellets, but a slice of hay. Stuffing the hay into the hay net in the far corner of the pen, she managed to get close enough to Blaze to unclasp the lead rope from her halter so that she was free to go and feed.

"I think we've done enough for one day, hey, girl?" Issie spoke gently to the mare. But inside she wasn't feeling so great about her first meeting with her new horse. How was she expected to feel when Blaze wouldn't even let her pat her?

She stood and watched as the mare nervously ate her hay. One thing was certain: this wasn't going to be easy.

CHAPTER 7

"Issie! Issie! I've got to talk to you..." Stella was panting from the effort of trying to catch up with her friend as she entered the school hall. It was Tuesday, assembly day, and they were late as always.

"Quick," Stella grabbed Issie by her school jersey as she caught her up, "let's sit up the back so we can talk."

She pushed through the herds of Chevalier Point High students trying to find seats and made a beeline for the back benches, dragging Issie along behind her. "Here!" Stella squeaked, claiming two spaces on a bench at the far end of the hall by throwing herself down and using her bag to mark a place next to her for Issie.

"So," she grinned as Issie sat down, "I know you don't want to talk about horses any more, but this isn't just about horses. It's like a mystery or something..." She paused for dramatic effect, lowering her voice to a whisper. "There's this new pony grazing at the pony-club paddocks and no one knows who it belongs to!"

Issie tried to speak, but before she could open her mouth Stella was rambling on again. "You should see this horse, Issie, she's beautiful. Part Arab I think, well, she looks like an Arab anyway. She's sort of a dark chestnut colour with a pale mane and tail, and white socks, totally gorgeous. She's really skinny and stuff but apart from that she's, like, the most amazing horse you've ever seen." Stella paused for just a minute to take a breath and then started raving on again.

"I've asked everyone at the pony club and no one seems to know who owns her. Kate thinks maybe she belongs to Natasha—"

"No she doesn't!" Issie snapped, fed up with Stella's chatter. "She belongs to me. She's mine."

"What?" Stella squealed. Instead of shutting her up it seemed that this news had her more excited than ever before.

"Why didn't you tell me? Issie! Where did she come from? How could you possibly afford her? Did your mum cave in and buy her for you after all? What's her name?"

"Her name is Blaze," Issie muttered under her breath. She could see Mrs Savage, the fourth form dean, glaring at her now. If they kept on talking during assembly then she and Stella were bound to get detention. "And Mum doesn't even know about her. I can't tell you any more now. It's too complicated. I'll explain after assembly – at lunch break."

At lunchtime, Issie was on her way to the tuck shop to get a fruit pie when she was almost tackled from behind. "Gotcha!" Stella giggled, her arms around Issie's waist. "Now, come on. Tell me what's going on. I'm not letting go until you do."

And so Issie told Stella the whole story – how Avery had found Blaze in a terrible state and brought her to Issie, who had agreed to take on the chestnut mare and nurse her back to health.

"And the worst thing is, she just doesn't trust people," Issie said. "Avery said I can ride her soon because she's putting on weight, but I don't want to rush things… It took me a week before she would let me brush the mud off her! She's been so scared, Stella!"

"Oh, Issie, how dreadful!" Stella's eyes brimmed with tears. "Poor Blaze. She must have been so badly mistreated by her old owners. That's why she's being so difficult. I'm sure you'll make friends with her if you just keep trying. You can't give up on her. She needs you."

Stella was buzzing with excitement. "I can't believe you've been keeping Blaze to yourself all this time too! We've got to go and find Kate and tell her all about it. She's been dying to discover who owned the mystery horse. We'll both meet you at the paddock after school."

When Stella and Kate arrived later that afternoon Issie had already caught Blaze and was tying her to the fence, preparing to groom her.

"She's beautiful!" Stella was breathless with admiration. It was the first time the girls had seen Blaze up close and even cool Kate was impressed.

"She's got wonderful conformation," she admitted as she ran her eye over the mare's elegant arched neck, "and what a gorgeous face with that fantastic white blaze! Blaze is the perfect name for her."

"You're right, Issie, she must be part Arab," Stella agreed. "Look at her lovely dished nose. I wonder if she has breeder's papers?"

"I don't know," Issie said. "We don't even know who her old owners were, so there's no way of finding out what her bloodlines are."

"Who could be so cruel, treating a horse like that?" Kate shook her head. "Does Avery have any leads to find the old owners?"

"Not yet," Issie said, "but he's reported it to the police so they might come up with something. Anyway," Issie turned to Blaze, "you're safe with me now, girl; I'm going to take good care of you."

"Well," Stella said, "I think it's time for Blaze to meet the boys." She turned to Kate. "Come on, let's go catch Toby and Coco and do some proper introductions."

The two girls grabbed their halters out of the tack room and set out across the paddock, leaving Issie alone again with Blaze.

"Good girl," Issie cooed, reaching out to stroke the mare on her neck. But Blaze made a low snorting sound and quickly backed away. Issie knew better by now than to be disappointed by the mare's behaviour. It was nothing personal; she understood that. Blaze's last owners were cruel to her, so why should she trust anyone?

Issie had been taking it slowly with the mare, trying to gain her trust. Now, as she moved towards Blaze, she didn't pick up a brush straight away. Instead, she reached out an open hand and stroked her wither. The chestnut leapt away at first, but as Issie tried again and again she finally stood still, letting the girl run her hands gently across her glossy neck, back over the wither and down her front legs, feeling tendon and fetlock, then back up again and along her rump and hindquarters, softly talking to the mare as she went.

All the time, Issie kept her gaze low and never looked Blaze in the eye. The stroking was something she had learnt in Avery's natural horsemanship classes.

Avery had also told her to keep her eyes down – horses are prey animals, and being met by the stare of a human predator was liable to spook them.

By the time Issie lifted up the dandy brush, she was thrilled to see that Blaze was almost relaxed under her hands. In fact, once Issie had scuffed the caked mud off her hocks and began to work on her with the body brush, the mare even seemed to enjoy the feeling of the soft bristles against her skin. When Issie took a thick, damp sponge and ran it down the white stripe in the middle of her forehead, Blaze gave a grunt of pleasure and lowered her head against Issie, using the girl as her scratching post, rubbing up and down against her.

"Hey," Issie giggled. "Cut it out!" But inside she was pleased to see Blaze acting so friendly with her. She was starting to trust her.

"Hey, Issie," Stella said as she led Coco up, tying her to the fence next to Blaze, "do you know those men?"

"What men?"

"Over there," Stella said, "in that white van. There are two of them. They've been sitting there watching us ever since we arrived. I thought they must have a flat tyre or something, but they haven't got out of the van to fix it. They're just sitting there staring at us. It's kinda creepy."

Issie put down her hoof-pick and turned around to take a look. Sure enough, there was a white van parked out on the kerb of the road. Two men sat silently in the front seat.

"What are you looking at?" Kate led Toby over to join them.

"That van over there," Stella said, pointing towards where the two men were parked.

Suddenly there was the sound of an engine revving up, and the white van did a quick u-turn back up the street and was gone.

"Well, they sure left in a hurry!" Kate was puzzled. "Who were they anyway?"

"Never mind," Stella chirped, "let's ride." She looked over at Issie who was still combing out Blaze's mane. "C'mon Issie. Are you going to tack her up or not?"

"I... I don't think she's ready to be ridden yet," Issie said. Although she knew that the *truth* was she wasn't ready yet. She was still nervous about getting up on the chestnut mare for the first time, and she certainly didn't want to do it with Stella and Kate watching her.

"Besides," Issie added, "Mum doesn't know I'm here and I'd better get home before she starts to worry."

"Issie, why haven't you just told her?" Kate was shocked.

"I will, I will. I'm just waiting for the right moment," Issie said.

The problem with this secret, though, was that it never seemed like the right time to share it. Every afternoon as she cycled home from the horse paddock Issie imagined herself telling her mother all about Blaze. But somehow, by the time she arrived home, her resolve to share her secret had faded. *Not just yet*, she thought. *Soon. When I've nursed Blaze back to health and we've made friends. Then Mum will have to let me keep her.*

And Blaze was getting healthy fast. In the short time that she had been at the River Paddock, the slender chestnut had put on condition at such a pace that her ribs no longer showed and her coat had lost its stark quality and was beginning to shine a deep burnished gold.

But it was the change in Blaze's mood that mattered most. When Issie arrived at the River Paddock late one afternoon after school she found the mare with her head over the fence of the pen looking almost pleased to see her.

It had been three weeks now since the chestnut mare had been gifted into Issie's care. Now when Issie tethered her to the fence paling, the mare didn't flinch or jump under her touch. Her confidence in Issie had grown. She had begun to trust her.

"What do you think, girl? Shall I take you for a ride?" Issie buried her face in Blaze's thick flaxen mane. She never thought she would want to get back on a horse after what happened to Mystic. But when she looked at Blaze now she suddenly felt this deep, strong urge. She wanted to ride again.

Then she suddenly realised – what was she going to ride her with? Mystic's saddle had been crushed in the accident. And since her mother still didn't even know that Blaze existed, she could hardly ask her to buy her a new one! "Looks like we're going bareback for now, girl." Issie smiled at Blaze.

She could use Mystic's old bridle. It had a simple Eggbutt snaffle bit; just right for Blaze. But before the chestnut mare could wear it, it would need some adjustments. Her pretty Arab face was much smaller, more dished than Mystic's solid features. Issie moved the cheek straps up a couple of holes and adjusted the cavesson noseband to match. Then she eased the bridle over Blaze's head to check the fit. Perfect.

Issie grabbed her old spare helmet out of the tack room and, leading Blaze by the reins, she guided her out of the pen and positioned the mare so that she was standing parallel to the fence. Then she climbed up on the railings and threw herself lightly on to her back.

As soon as Issie mounted Blaze the thought struck her: *What if this mare is actually unbroken? What if I'm sitting on a wild horse who has never had a rider on her back before?*

Her fears disappeared as Blaze accepted her weight and the feel of the bit in her mouth.

"Let's go, girl!" Issie clucked the mare on and

gave her a dig with her heels. Blaze snorted and shot forward at a smart high-stepping trot, which almost rocked Issie off her back.

As Blaze trotted briskly on, Issie found herself sliding around. Riding bareback could be slippery. Without stirrups Issie couldn't rise to the trot, and the bouncing made it almost impossible to stay on.

Holding on to a handful of mane, Issie wrapped her legs firmly around the mare and tried not to jiggle like a jelly as she trotted on. Steering was nearly impossible and it was all she could do to point Blaze towards the entrance to the dressage ring.

Too late she realised that the chestnut was going too far to the left. She tried to pull Blaze to a halt, but the sudden tug on the reins made her bolt forward, missing the entrance entirely. Instead of slowing down, Blaze broke into a canter and headed for the gate that led to the far paddock.

"It's OK," Issie told herself, "the gate is shut. She's bound to stop." But Blaze showed no signs of slowing down, in fact her canter increased in speed. Issie found herself completely out of control, her hands tangled in the flaxen mane as she struggled to stay on board.

"My God! She's going to take the gate!" Issie couldn't believe it. The gate between the two main paddocks must have been at least one metre twenty high and Blaze was racing at it in full canter, completely ignoring Issie's frantic tugs on the reins. With her head held high, Blaze was fighting the bit, and Issie didn't have the strength to haul her back.

A few strides out from the gate, Blaze gave a proud toss of her head, freeing herself from the reins, and then leapt. The chestnut mare arched tidily through the air, clearing the gate with room to spare, and Issie lost her grip on the mane and began to slide. As Blaze landed lightly on the other side of the fence Issie landed too – heavily on the ground with a thud.

The long grass helped cushion her fall. Still, she felt a jolt of pain in her shoulder, and it took her a minute to get her breath back.

As she got up and wiped the dirt off her jodhpurs Issie was shaking and tears of anger and frustration welled up in her eyes. She should never have been so cocky, she realised. After all she'd never ridden Blaze before. She had no idea what this horse was capable of. And yet there she went, as bold as brass, climbing on board and trotting off as if she were the world's best rider. Well, she had paid the price for it. She straightened up, giving her limbs a shake to check that everything was in working order, and looked around for Blaze, who already had her head down munching a patch of long grass as if nothing had ever happened.

Why had Avery given her this horse? It was obvious that Blaze was too spirited for her to ride. She had overestimated herself. She should never have given up on her vow.

"Maybe I'm really not meant to ride after all," she sighed, reaching for Blaze's reins. She led the mare back to the pen on foot, not willing to suffer another fall on the way home. Then she unbridled Blaze, gave her some feed and refilled the hay net and cycled home, her head stuck in a cloud of gloomy thoughts.

She should have known better than to take on this horse; she realised that now. Blaze was moody and unpredictable, not at all what she was used to. If only Mystic were still alive. With Mystic, it had all been easy, she had known what to do. The little grey had been so sweet, like her best friend. With Blaze, it was like she couldn't do anything right. In fact, the mare didn't even seem to like her!

Was it too late to change her mind, she wondered, and give the horse back to Avery? Issie knew the answer. Avery would probably take Blaze back but he would be so disappointed in her she wouldn't be able to stand it. No, she had to stick at it. Things would get better with Blaze. They had to.

CHAPTER 8

"Isadora! Wait! What is that sticking out through your shirt?"

It was a quarter to four. Issie had just charged in through the front door to make herself a sandwich and change into her riding gear before heading out to see Blaze. She hadn't counted on running into her mum. Or that her new body piercing would be so visible through the thin white weave of her school shirt.

"Ummm…" Issie wasn't sure what to say. Lying to her mother would probably just make things worse. Best to tell the truth and get it over and done with.

"It's a belly-button ring. I got it done a couple of weeks ago," Issie admitted.

"What? What were you thinking? Let me see it!" Mrs Brown made Issie pull up her shirt to show her navel, still red and puffy from where the ring had pierced the skin. "Oh, Issie! Why didn't you talk to me before you had this done? Look at it! It could get infected!" Mrs Brown was furious.

"It's only a belly-button ring, everyone's got them these days," Issie stood her ground.

"You know very well that you don't charge off and do things like that without talking to me first," Mrs Brown countered. "Honestly, Isadora. Since your father left it hasn't been easy looking after you by myself. But at least I always thought I could rely on you to behave like a grown-up. And now you go off and do this! I'm really disappointed in you."

"It just sort of happened," Issie tried to explain. "Stella was having hers done and—"

"Stella! I might have known." Mrs Brown was livid. "And I suppose if Stella was jumping off a bridge you'd be racing off to do that too, would you?" she snapped. "For God's sake, Isadora, I thought you had more common sense. I hope you checked the equipment they used was sterilised? Heaven knows what diseases you could get from this. Where did you get it done?"

"At Lacey's chemist. Penny went with us."

Mrs Brown calmed down a little. "Well, even so, that doesn't automatically make it safe. There's still a chance that you could get an infection or blood poisoning. Have you been putting antiseptic on it?"

Issie nodded quietly.

"Isadora, I just wish you would talk to me before you race off and do these things, OK?" Mrs Brown fretted. "There are some decisions that are too important to make on your own."

Issie took a deep breath. Now was obviously not the time to tell her mother about Blaze. After all, if she thought Issie was irresponsible getting her belly button pierced without her permission then how would she feel if she knew her daughter had gone ahead and agreed to look after a new pony without even asking her?

Mrs Brown gave her daughter a stern look. "You realise I should probably punish you for this, don't you? It looks like you'll be spending your time after school helping me out at the office so I can keep an eye on you."

Issie's blood ran cold. This couldn't be happening. If her mum dragged her in to work with her every afternoon then how on earth was she going to get to the horse paddock to look after Blaze? With just a few weeks of school left before the summer holidays, Issie had been counting the days until she was free to spend more time with her horse. Until then, she could only sneak away for a couple of hours each day after school. And now she wouldn't even be able to do that!

"No, Mum!" she squeaked. "Please don't. I won't ever do anything like this again. I promise. I was going to ask you first, only Stella made me go there straight away and... oh, Mum, please don't ground me, please!"

"Well," Mrs Brown considered, "I really don't know..." She furrowed her brow and let out a deep sigh, examining her daughter's pleading face. "OK, OK. But I don't want to see you walking through that door with any more body piercings, is that clear, young lady? I want no more surprises out of you."

"Oh, thanks, Mum!" Issie gushed, giving her a hug before bounding up the stairs.

Five minutes later she reappeared again in a sweatshirt and jeans.

"Where on earth are you off to now?" Mrs Brown asked.

"I won't be long," Issie said as she headed for the door. "I'm, umm… going down to the paddock to help Kate pull Toby's mane."

"All right, but be back in time for dinner. No later than seven, OK?" her mother yelled after her.

No more suprises? What would happen if her mum found out about Blaze? Issie thought about how she had lied to her mum. She felt bad not telling her about Blaze, but the time wasn't right. Not yet. For now, the horse had to be her secret.

Kate and Stella were in the tack room when Issie arrived at the River Paddock. "I can't find them anywhere!" Stella was grumbling as she rummaged through a pile of numnahs and old blankets on the floor.

"Find what?" Issie asked.

"The keys to the paddock gates," Stella said. "You

know how we always keep a spare set here in case we need to undo the padlock and get the horses out? Well they're missing. And not only that, when I came down to the paddock this afternoon the tack room was wide open – and I could have sworn I locked it last night!"

"Maybe another rider was here after you and they left the tack room open?" suggested Kate as she straightened up the messy pile of horse blankets that Stella had strewn everywhere.

"Anyway," Stella sighed, "the keys to the paddock are gone. What are we going to do? I wanted to go ride out today."

"Let's saddle up," Kate said briskly. "We don't even need to leave the River Paddock. We can head down to the back paddock and take a ride through The Pines."

The Pines were a glade of tall pine trees at the far end of the back paddock. In winter the ground there was boggy, but in summer it was perfect for riding. A dirt track ran between the trees, scattered with pine cones and covered in a thick blanket of dark brown pine needles, which filled the air with their fresh scent.

The Pines had been Mystic's special place. Issie

had loved cantering him through the cool of the trees on a hot summer day. But she wasn't so sure about Blaze. The path between the trees was narrow with low branches over it, hard to navigate on such a headstrong mare.

"Ummm, I don't think Blaze is ready for that," Issie had to admit.

"Oh, go on, it'll be OK," Stella insisted. "We'll go at the front so she can follow us."

The three girls set off at a trot towards the far paddock, Stella and Kate posting up and down, while Issie bounced along bareback. The weeks spent without a saddle had done wonders for Issie's seat and even at a quick trot she felt secure on Blaze's sleek back. As they got near The Pines she even forgot her fears and felt a surge of excitement at the idea of cantering through them again.

The back paddock dropped away down a grassy slope to the trees and the girls trotted down until they reached the path into The Pines. "Ready to canter?" Stella shouted back as she kicked Coco on, leaning forward and standing up in her stirrups so that her weight was out of the saddle.

Issie waited for Coco and Toby to go on ahead before clucking Blaze on to canter. But the mare was suddenly struck with fear at being left behind by her new friends. When Issie urged her on into a gentle canter, she sprang forward as if she was a racehorse in a starting gate, not at a canter, but in full gallop.

"Blaze, stop it, girl! No!" Issie pulled back hard on the reins, but Blaze was having none of it. She had set the bit between her teeth and was off.

At a canter The Pines were easy enough to ride through, but at full gallop with no saddle? Impossible. Worse still, as Blaze strained against the reins, her speed increasing, she began to gain quickly on the horses ahead of her. There was no way the path was wide enough for Blaze to pass the other horses – she would crash into them for sure.

"Out of the way!" Issie yelled to the riders ahead of her. "Blaze is out of control. She won't stop!"

In front of her, Kate and Stella had heard the sound of hoofbeats before they even heard Issie's cries. Now, they urged their horses on. There was no room for them to pull over to the side of the path, and no time to stop. The best option was to ride hard and try to make it to the opening at the other end of The Pines before Issie caught up with them.

The fiery Arab was still ignoring Issie's attempts to slow her down, lost in the pleasure of her own speed. Her strides ate up the ground in front of her, and she was gaining quickly on Toby and Coco.

"Whoa now, girl!" Issie fought to keep her balance and grabbed up a handful of mane with the reins, pulling back as hard as she could. Blaze gave a rebellious snort and kept on running. In front of her, Coco was heaving with the effort of keeping up the pace, her coat flecked with sweat.

At a gallop the three horses emerged from the pine trees into the green clearing on the other side, and as Toby and Coco moved quickly out of the way Blaze powered forward, still in full gallop.

It wasn't until Issie had reached the far end of the paddock that she was finally able to slow the mare down a little, first to a canter, then a trot and finally a gentle jog. Even though her sides were heaving from the run, Issie had to keep a tight hold on her horse to stop her from bolting off again.

"Steady, girl, good girl, Blaze," she breathed, her

arms trembling from the effort of hanging on to the reins. Her heart was beating like a drum in her ears.

"That was amazing!" Kate yelled out as she rode towards her. "I've never seen a horse run like that. Toby's an ex-racehorse and Blaze even gave him a run for his money."

"Good on you for staying on her back at that speed!" Stella was obviously impressed. Issie, however, was less pleased.

"This is the second time she's got away on me." Issie was shaking. "I just can't control her. It's like she goes crazy the minute I get on her back."

Issie had been expecting sympathy from her friends, so she was shocked when Stella barked at her instead, "You're being silly, Issie! Everyone knows you're a natural rider. That's why Avery chose you to take Blaze on. OK, so she's being difficult. I'm sure all she needs to sort her out is a little bit of proper schooling. Talk to Tom. After all, he gave her to you. So why don't you ask him for a little help?"

Stella was right, of course. Issie had been trying to struggle on alone. What she really needed was some advice. "I'll ask Tom if he'll meet me at the paddock one day next week when the holidays have started to give me a hand." Issie nodded. "He'll know what to do."

Still, deep-down she doubted that anyone could really help her ride this spirited mare. Was Blaze too much horse for her to handle?

In the darkness of her bedroom that night, Issie had the dream again. It always began in the same way. The rhythmic sound of hoofbeats seemed to thunder out from the blackness and then the horse appeared like a silver mist in the gloom. As he came closer Issie could make out the misty outline of his body, the proud arch of his neck crested with a thick mane, and the long sweep of his elegant silver tail which trailed almost to the ground. The horse gave a soft nicker and came closer. He was just a few metres away now and Issie could see him clearly at last. It was Mystic. His dark-rimmed eyes looked at Issie intently and he was still for a moment. Then he pawed the ground and gave an agitated shake of his mane, before breaking into a high-stepping trot and heading straight for her.

Mystic came to an abrupt stop right in front of Issie. She reached out a hand to touch him, but before she could get near enough Mystic went up, rearing on his hind legs so that his front hooves thrashed the air above her. At the same time he let out a terrible long, low squeal – the noise a stallion might make if he was rounding up his herd against danger. It was a sound so deep and piercing that it woke Issie up with a start. She sat bolt upright in bed, her heart racing, her pyjamas damp with sweat.

Even now, wide awake, she could still hear Mystic's shrill squeal ringing in her ears. And then she heard something else. Not a squeal, but the drumming of hoofbeats. It sounded to Issie as if the noise were coming from just outside her bedroom window. Without hesitating she leapt up and raced to pull back the curtains, squinting out into the darkness.

She stood quietly at the window and held her breath as she tried hard to listen again. Nothing. The night air was completely still. Her eyes had adjusted now and she could see that the back yard was empty. Reluctantly, Issie let the curtain drop from her hand, moved away from the window and slipped back under the covers and into bed. It was all a dream, she told herself. But as she drifted back off to sleep she could have sworn she still heard the sound of hoofbeats somewhere out there in the darkness.

CHAPTER 9

"Why, Issie! She's looking brilliant, isn't she?" Avery was obviously thrilled at the sight of the chestnut mare.

Blaze was a different horse from the one that had arrived at the River Paddock one late spring morning. She had blossomed under Issie's tender care. She had put on condition so that her ribs no longer stood out so much, and her liver chestnut coat, previously patchy and dull, had been groomed until it gleamed like precious metal.

"I've been giving her a mix of oats, crushed barley and chaff to fatten her up a bit, and a dose of linseed oil to put a shine on her coat," Issie said proudly.

"Fantastic!" Avery enthused as he ran a hand over Blaze's rump, checking on her condition. "Well done. But I can see why this mare has been giving you trouble. Arabs are notoriously hotheaded sorts, and if this girl has been getting pepped up on a diet of oats and the like she's probably got too much energy for her own good. Now that she's in better shape we'll have to cut out the oats to calm her down.

"Now," Avery said, looking around, "let's get started. Where's your gear?" Issie reminded Avery that her saddle had been destroyed in the accident with Mystic. "Well," Avery considered, "not to worry. We won't be needing a saddle for this lesson anyway." He cast a glance at his watch. "At least you're here," he grumbled and reached out a hand to give Issie a leg up. "Where are the other two? I told them to be here at precisely two o'clock—"

The sound of hooves on gravel interrupted him.

"Wait for us!" squeaked Kate, trotting briskly along the road towards the fields.

"We're really sorry we're late!" Stella added. Her chubby little mare was heaving with the effort of keeping up with Kate's rangy Thoroughbred.

"Well, it looks like you've more than warmed these two up," Avery snapped. "Come on then. Let's spend a few minutes in the arena getting them to accept the bit and then we'll pop them over a few jumps and check out your positions."

As they entered the arena Blaze took the lead. "Issie," Avery said, "you change the rein and keep her moving at a steady walk, then when you get into the far corner ask her to move into a trot. Keep plenty of leg on her and keep your hands nice and still."

"You two," he gestured to Kate and Stella, "follow along behind Blaze. Come on, girls! I want to see these ponies paying attention."

As they worked the horses in around the arena, Avery busied himself in the middle of the ring, setting up trotting poles and cavalletti. "Right. Kate, you take the lead now and go over this combination that I've set up," Avery instructed. "The rest of you follow along behind Kate, leaving a decent space between you."

Kate and Stella went on ahead, taking the trotting poles with ease. But as Issie circled Blaze to follow them the mare tossed her head up, avoiding the bit and looking wild-eyed at the rails.

"Keep her steady, Isadora," Avery said.

But it was no use. Blaze simply wasn't paying her any attention. She took the trotting poles with an ungainly bound, then raced at the first cavalletti, throwing Issie back and almost unseating her. Landing off balance, Issie clutched on to the mare's mane as she stopped dead in front of the last jump, then changed her mind and bunny-hopped across it. Issie lurched forward, still hanging on as Blaze took the jump. But as they landed she couldn't keep her balance any longer, and flew over her horse's head.

Hitting the ground with a thud, Issie tried to relax, knowing that it was better to let her body absorb the impact. Still, she felt herself gasping for air as the wind was knocked out of her, and it took a minute or two before she could get her breath back and stand up. By the time she was on her feet, Avery was heading towards her, leading Blaze by the reins.

"Are you OK?" he asked as he reached her. "Yeah, I'm fine, just totally embarrassed," Issie wanted to say. Instead, she just nodded.

"Well, too many oats certainly have made Blaze a bit hot." Avery smiled at her. At least he didn't think she fell off because she was a useless rider!

Issie brushed herself down and tried to calm her nerves with a deep breath as Avery offered a hand to give her a leg up.

He turned to Kate and Stella: "Girls, I know you were looking forward to having a lesson but I think we need to focus on Blaze today. Why don't you unsaddle and then you can come back over to the arena and watch us?"

He turned to Issie: "We need to take things back to basics with Blaze," he told her. "I know you've been along to one or two of my natural horsemanship classes in the past, but with the problems you've been having with Blaze, I think it's time for some special advanced lessons."

He took the mare by the reins and looked at his pupil. "You can dismount now," he said.

Issie was confused. "But, I thought… I thought you just said we were going to do some more work…"

"A natural horseman knows that if you want to be a good rider, the first step is learning to handle your horse while you're still on the ground," Avery replied. "Then once you have your horse's trust and respect you can do anything you like. Now take Blaze into the middle of the arena. We'll play some training games with her that will get her listening to you, and then we'll get started on the real work."

If you happened to see Issie that afternoon playing her natural horsemanship games you would think she looked pretty silly: jumping up and down in front of her horse, waggling her arms and legs like a crazy puppet on a string; doing star jumps in front of Blaze with a pair of plastic shopping bags billowing in her hands, followed by another set of star jumps, this time with a raincoat in one hand and an old umbrella in the other. There were moments when it all seemed so ridiculous that even Issie fell about laughing.

But Avery would glare at her and remind her that this was serious business. "These games are designed to make Blaze 'bombproof'. Do you know what that means?"

"I think so," Issie said. "It means a horse who behaves well no matter what."

"Exactly. We want Blaze to have so much faith in you that nothing can scare her."

And with that, he gave Issie a leg up on to Blaze's back. "That's enough groundwork. Time for you to put your faith in Blaze for once," he said. Avery reached up and undid the throatlash and noseband, lifted the reins forward over Blaze's ears and then slipped the bridle off her head.

"But... what are you doing? How am I supposed to ride if she hasn't got a bridle on?" Issie squeaked.

"You don't need one," Avery insisted. "Just hang on to a handful of mane and sit there. We're going to let Blaze steer. She can go anywhere she wants. I just want you to sit tight and let her have her head."

Avery stood with his arm around Blaze's neck, calming the mare while Issie got comfortable. She gripped a thick hank of mane in her hands and wrapped her legs tightly around Blaze's sleek body.

"No, no, don't grip up with your legs. Relax a little," Avery instructed. "If you relax, your horse will relax too. Now, I'm going to let her go and I want you to just sit there. That's right. Stay perfectly still and let her decide for herself where to go." He kept talking as he released his grip on Blaze. "Horses are used to being told what to do by their riders. So naturally, if you ask one to think by itself for a change, suddenly their brains start to work and, well, who knows what could happen."

"I could fall off again, that's what could happen..." Issie muttered.

"The rails of the dressage arena will keep her from going too far," Avery pointed out. "Now, just sit there and relax totally."

Issie tried to relax but it wasn't easy. Blaze was all excited by the weight of a rider on her back. Her ears were pricked forward and her head was held high. She launched herself into a high-stepping trot and let out a shrill whinny as she charged down to the far end of the dressage arena. Issie forgot about relaxing and concentrated on hanging on as Blaze turned sharply and trotted back up the side of the arena.

"She's doing well," Avery coached. "She's just starting to understand that she can do whatever she likes. In a moment she'll calm down and start walking." Issie wasn't so sure. Any minute now, Blaze could realise that she was free and take a flying leap over the rails of the arena instead, dumping Issie in the process. The trot had now become a canter and Blaze seemed confused by the combination of the weight on her back and no bit in her mouth to control her. She gave a snort and shook her head.

"Stay calm, she'll settle down." Avery insisted.

And he was right. Blaze stopped cantering all by herself, slowing down to a gentle jog. She trotted on, snorting and breathing heavily through her nostrils. "That blowing means she's nice and relaxed," Avery said. "Now try to guide her with your legs, make her trot from one side of the arena to the other."

Issie gently touched Blaze's left side with her leg and felt the mare startle underneath her. She hadn't expected the horse to charge forward so suddenly.

"That's good," Avery reassured her. "Blaze is so alert you only need to give her the lightest of aids. Try again."

This time Blaze responded perfectly as Issie pushed her gently forwards, trotting smoothly across the ring.

"And back again," Avery commanded.

Again, Blaze obeyed perfectly and Issie began to feel the thrill of controlling this wild, high-spirited mare with nothing more than the lightest touch. Riding free, with no saddle or bridle to bind them, she felt as if she were almost a part of the magnificent chestnut Arab beneath her. For the first time since Mystic's death she felt that wonderful feeling again – the sensation that she and her horse were one and the same, the perfect team.

"Now circle around to the end of the ring," Avery continued. "And you can take Blaze over that jump that I've constructed for you."

Issie felt a tingle of nerves. One time at pony club they had knotted their reins and jumped with no hands over a low fence. But never without a saddle or bridle. How could she possibly control Blaze?

"You won't have to control her," Avery read her mind. "Just let her go and stay with her. Blaze loves to jump; she'll do all the work."

The jump Avery had constructed was made out of forty-four gallon drums lying on their side, topped off with a red and white striped rail. Issie had jumped that high before – but never bareback and certainly not without a bridle to steer with. She stared at the jump, her stomach churning with butterflies, as Blaze circled around it.

"Don't look down at the ground," Avery shouted. "Look up and over the fence, otherwise Blaze will refuse to jump. That's it! Now stay relaxed and turn her towards me."

At the sight of the jump, Blaze's ears pricked forward and she broke into a canter. "Good girl, steady girl." Issie tried to stay relaxed, guiding her horse on and keeping her steady with her legs until she had almost reached the fence. Then she took a fistful of mane in each hand and held her breath. Blaze didn't just jump the fence – she flew over it. Issie felt the surge of power as the mare sprang lightly into the air, and the thrill of landing cleanly on the other side of the fence. They had done it!

"I can't believe it! She jumped it!" Issie gave Blaze a huge slappy pat on her neck. "It was like flying." She had a grin from ear to ear. Stella and Kate, who had been watching the whole thing, were clapping and whooping on the sidelines.

Blaze, too, was buzzing with pleasure. She pranced lightly from side to side, obviously keen to take the fence again.

Avery held the mare still as Issie dismounted. "Well

done, you two." He smiled at his pupil. "That's what natural horsemanship is all about. A horse and rider working as a team. Remember," he told her, "if you have a good seat you don't need to rely on a saddle or bridle. You know Vaughn Jefferis? He's one of New Zealand's most famous eventing riders – he has a fantastic seat – and he learnt to ride bareback. It took four years before his dad finally realised he was serious about being a competitive rider and bought him a saddle. That's why he has such perfect balance when he rides a cross-country course – he's totally in touch with his horse."

Avery looked at Issie. "Your riding has improved more than you realise over the past month since you've been riding Blaze. You two make quite a team now." Avery continued, "In fact, I think you're both ready to come along to the rally this weekend."

"Really?" Issie was shocked; it seemed too soon to take the mare on a pony-club outing, but if Avery was convinced that she was up to it…

"That's settled then," he said briskly, turning and walking off towards his truck. Then he span on his heels to face Issie: "Oh, and one more thing – when you arrive at the club grounds on Sunday, meet me at the horse truck. I've got a surprise for you."

"Another surprise?" Issie squawked. What on earth did Avery have in store for her this time?

CHAPTER 10

As she rode Blaze through the gates of the Chevalier Point Pony Club grounds Issie felt a twinge of embarrassment. It was only a rally day, but even so, all of the ponies would be nicely turned out, with their gear polished and oiled. And here she was riding without even a saddle!

Not only that, Blaze was still totally unpredictable. What if she decided to act up and Issie found herself falling off in front of the whole club? A million thoughts were racing through Issie's head – none of them good. After all, the last time she rode here had been a disaster, a disaster that had ended with Mystic's death.

"Stay calm or you'll pass your nerves on to your horse," Issie told herself firmly. Certainly Blaze seemed happy enough as they entered the grounds. Issie trotted her up to where the horse floats were parked and headed to her usual tethering spot under one of the massive plane trees. It was going to be a scorcher of a day and the big plane would shade Blaze from the heat of the sun.

The smell of privet flower filled the warm morning air. It was still early, around nine a.m., but already there were over a dozen riders here, tacking up their horses and preparing for the rally.

Issie dismounted and slipped Blaze's halter on over the top of her bridle, tying her to the nearby fence. "I won't be gone long, girl, I promise." Issie gave Blaze a quick pat on the neck and headed for the clubrooms. There was time to grab a cold Coke out of the drinks machine before the rally began.

As she reached the clubroom steps Issie looked back over her shoulder to check on her pony. Blaze seemed happy enough. She was standing peacefully under the trees with eyes half closed in a doze, resting one hind leg and swatting the summer flies away with her pale golden tail.

Issie was so busy looking at her horse that she didn't notice another girl racing down the steps as she was going up them. The two of them ran headfirst into one another and a mug of tea went flying.

"Watch where you're going, you stupid cow!" snapped the girl.

Issie looked up and saw Natasha Tucker, her white riding shirt soaked with tea, her face set in a vicious scowl.

"I'm so sorry!" Issie said.

"My shirt is ruined," Natasha snipped. "Calvin Klein! Ruined."

"I'm really sorry," Issie apologised again. "Have you got something else to wear for the rest of the day? We could try rinsing it off under the tap by the horse trough—"

"Yeah, what-ever." Natasha rolled her eyes, obviously losing interest in the whole conversation. "I'll give it to Mum; she can sort it out. Say..." she peered at Issie carefully, "don't you ride that old grey pony? That's your horse, isn't it? But I thought he was..."

"Hit by a truck. Yes..." Issie felt her lips start to tremble. She was determined not to let the thought of

Mystic upset her. She didn't want to lose it in front of Natasha. She wouldn't understand.

"He was killed in the accident," Issie said matter-of-factly. "I'm riding a new horse now." She pointed to Blaze who was standing under the trees with her rump towards them.

"What? That skinny bag of bones!" Natasha said. "She doesn't look up to much."

"Actually," Issie felt her blood boiling, "she's got an amazing jump in her. I was riding her the other day and we went clean over the gate between the two paddocks where I graze her. And she hasn't even been properly schooled yet. I'm sure she'd make a great showjumper with a bit more work."

Issie didn't mean to boast but she just couldn't help herself. She couldn't stand the way Natasha was so smug. Besides, she wasn't exactly fibbing – Blaze did jump over the gate. Issie just didn't mention the fact that it was all Blaze's idea and all *she* did was fall off.

"In fact," Issie continued, "I plan to train her up as an eventing mount. I'll be competing on her shortly."

"Oh, really?" Natasha smirked. "So you'll be riding

at the Chevalier Point one-day event next month, I suppose?"

"Oh, definitely. We're in training for it now," Issie lied.

"Me too," said Natasha. "Goldrush's last owner rode her to area trials and I expect to do the same, so this will be a warm-up competition for us..."

Natasha had been staring distractedly at Blaze while she spoke. Now she turned back to Issie. "Where's your saddle?"

"What?"

"Your saddle," repeated Natasha. "I don't see one on your horse. Where is it? You're not planning to ride her bareback at a one-day event are you?"

Issie didn't know what to say. It was no use lying about it because the rally was about to get underway and Natasha would soon see the truth for herself: that she didn't have a saddle, or any other gear for that matter.

"I, umm... the thing is..."

"Actually Isadora has two saddles. One for dressage and another for jumping and cross-country. We just weren't sure which one to tack Blaze up with for today, were we, Issie?" Tom Avery smiled as he stepped out of the clubrooms and stood beside the two girls.

"So what do you reckon, Issie? Shall we put the dressage saddle on her this morning then swap to the jumping saddle after lunch?"

Issie just nodded. She couldn't believe it. Tom to the rescue!

"Come on. I've got your tack in my truck; let's get her ready." Avery bounded down the stairs towards his horse truck and Issie gratefully followed, relieved to be getting away from Natasha.

She finally caught up with Avery just as he reached the truck. "Tom, thanks so much for covering up for me," Issie gasped, "it's just that Natasha is such a, well, a snob, I suppose, and if I'd told her that I really didn't have a saddle—" Tom cut Issie off in mid-sentence.

"Covering for you? I don't know what you're talking about, Isadora. I was telling Natasha the truth. I've got both your saddles right here in the cab. Can't have you riding bareback at a pony-club meet now, can we?"

Avery opened the front door of the horse truck, and there on the passenger seat of the truck cab sat two saddles. "Remember the other day I said I had a surprise for you?" Avery reached in and grabbed the nearest one. It was made of soft black leather, and had the deep seat and straight-cut flaps of a traditional dressage saddle. "It's a Bates Maestro," he said, handing it to her so that her arm slid through the gullet. "It used to be my eventing saddle. I've ridden dressage tests in this saddle in all the big competitions around the world – at Burghley, Badminton and Lexington. It'll be a tiny bit big for you, I suppose, but it has adjustable kneepads which will help, and we can alter the stirrups, of course. It should fit Blaze just fine. As should this one..."

Avery reached across the seat and lifted out the second saddle. It was made of dark tan leather and seemed more well worn than the first saddle; the kneepads were scuffed a little and there were sweat stains on the padding underneath. *Not surprising*, thought Issie – this was clearly Avery's cross-country saddle.

"This one was made especially for me." Avery stared at the saddle proudly. "It has a flat seat and the first time I rode a cross-country in it I swore I would fall off, but it's actually very comfortable compared to those old-fashioned deep-seated models. It's not ideal for the showjumping phase, but it does the trick.

"It's just the sort of saddle you'll be needing," he added, "if you're going to be riding Blaze at that one-day event."

Issie was stunned. Avery must have heard her entire conversation with Natasha, including all her boasting about entering the one-day event.

"I'm not really entering..." Issie began.

"But of course you are!" Avery boomed. "You've got the saddles. You've got the horse. What else do you need?"

"But I've never even ridden Blaze over a proper fence yet!" Issie protested.

"Nonsense," Avery said, "you said yourself she has a big jump in her. And from what I've seen I'd say this mare is no novice jumper. It looks to me like she's been well-schooled already in the past. All you need to do is bring out the best in her again.

"The one-day event isn't until the end of the season, so you've got nearly two months to train. You've already got her well fed and her fitness is improving. You'll have to commit yourself to training solidly every day from now until the event, of course, but you can do it. Now let's get this saddle on Blaze and see how it looks, shall we?"

For Issie, the rest of the day passed by in a sun-filled blur. There were around fifty riders in the Chevalier Point Pony Club – the best ten riders of the club being chosen to train with Avery. Issie was thrilled when she was singled out along with Kate, Stella, Dan and the dreaded Natasha to join Avery's group.

The morning was spent schooling the horses and Issie was amazed at her own progress. The weeks without a saddle had actually done her some good and she had developed an independent seat. Still, having a fabulous new saddle certainly helped and Blaze behaved like a perfect angel, trotting around the ring with her neck flexed and on the bit. Her paces seemed so light it was as if she didn't touch the ground, but floated around the arena.

It was nearly two in the afternoon by the time lunch break came, and Issie was exhausted and starving. She had just taken Blaze's bridle off and loosened her girth a little so she could relax, then thrown herself down on the long grass under the tree, when Dan appeared.

"Hey, no slacking off!" He grinned. "You're my new groom, remember?"

"What?" Issie didn't understand.

"We made a bet," Dan said, "at the gymkhana, remember? The loser had to groom the winner's horse for a week. Well, I'm ready to take you up on that now."

"I can't believe you!" Issie was shocked. "After all that happened to me that day you actually want me to come over and brush down your horse! God, Dan, you're so insensitive!"

"Hey, hey…" Dan's smile was gone. "I was just kidding, Issie. Honestly. I really came over to see if you want to join us for lunch. Mum's made a giant bacon and egg pie – it's too big for even me and Ben to finish off. And there's stacks of sandwiches and banana cake and…"

"I'd love to." Issie smiled, feeling foolish about her outburst. "Just let me tie Blaze up and I'll be right there."

On the grass beside the Halliday's horse float Dan's mum was laying out the picnic. "Isadora! It's so good to see you riding again!" Mrs Halliday smiled. "Where's your mother today?"

"Ummm, she had too much work on and couldn't make it," Issie said, silently thinking to herself that this must be her day for telling whopping great lies. First she fibbed to Natasha about entering the one-day event, and now she was lying to Mrs Halliday about her mum. The truth was, she still hadn't told her mother about Blaze. She had been too scared to mention it. And now, well, the longer she left it, the harder it seemed to confess that she had started riding again. And with her mum away at work all day, and no school for the rest of summer, it was easy for Issie to slip away each day to school Blaze without being found out.

"Would you like a slice of pie or a sandwich?" Mrs Halliday offered.

"Oh, Mum, give her both! It's been a tough day." Dan laughed, standing up and dusting off his jodhpurs. "I'm going to the drinks machine. Anyone else want anything?"

Issie shook her head and watched as Dan walked off to the clubrooms to get a drink. She watched as he ran up the steps and bumped into, of all people, Natasha Tucker. This time, though, Natasha didn't seem upset about banging into someone. Instead she let out a torrent of girlish laughter as Dan said something to her, and then she placed her hand softly on top of his as they chatted.

Seeing them together like that made Issie feel sick to her stomach. She'd never actually thought about Dan as a boyfriend or anything before, but now that she saw him smiling and laughing with Natasha, she realised she was more than a little jealous.

"God, she is such a flirt!" Issie muttered under her breath.

"What's that?" asked Ben, who was busily tucking into his third piece of bacon and egg pie.

"Uhh, nothing," Issie pulled herself together, "I was just wondering what we'll be doing first after lunch."

"They're setting up the games now so I suppose it will be bending and flag races," Ben said, sounding a little disappointed. "It's a shame really. I had been hoping to get in some jumping training."

"As if you need it!" Issie laughed. "I'm the one who needs the jumping training. I'm entering the one-day event."

"On Blaze?" Ben was shocked. "Well, you're right. You do need to train more than I do. Dan and I are already having lessons on Wednesday and Thursday with Tom. Why don't you join us? We meet here at the club grounds at four."

"That sounds great!" Issie agreed. This would give her a chance to prepare Blaze for the one-day event – and hang out with Dan at the same time. Life was definitely starting to improve, she decided as she took another egg sandwich and lay back on the grass with her eyes shut and the sun on her face.

CHAPTER 11

"Working Trot at K, proceed around the arena to H..." Tom Avery was reading instructions out loud from a piece of paper as Issie trotted Blaze around the dressage arena. There were just two weeks to go until the one-day event, and Avery was taking his squad one by one through a practice run of their dressage tests. For the big day the riders would have to know all the movements off by heart, but today he was reading the test out for them as they rode.

The dressage arena had been marked out with white boards, each one painted with a large capital letter. The letters were set up at various points around the ring and Issie had to make sure Blaze did exactly as she asked when she reached the right marker.

"At C, canter on in a twenty metre circle..." Avery's voice boomed across the ring.

Issie held Blaze lightly with her hands and asked her gently with seat and legs to move into a canter. The pretty chestnut needed only the subtlest of commands, she was so responsive. As she flew around the ring in a graceful canter, Issie could almost imagine she was competing at some huge event like the Badminton Horse Trials. She pictured Blaze with her blonde mane and tail perfectly plaited up, with tight white bandages over her white socks. And there she was on her back in tails and a top hat, entering the ring, saluting the judge...

"No, no, no! Wake up, Issie, you're not paying attention! You should be changing the rein at B across the arena!" Avery barked at her. "Change the rein, change the rein! Then turn up the middle at A, halt at X and leave the arena on a loose rein."

Issie woke up with a jolt and got back on track, trotting up the centre line beautifully to halt and salute with Blaze standing perfectly square and calm.

"If I keep daydreaming like this," Issie muttered to Blaze as they left the arena, "we'll never make it to the Chevalier Point one-day event, let alone Badminton."

Avery smiled at Issie as she pulled the chestnut mare up beside the other riders. "Well, apart from having a dilly dream for a rider, Blaze is doing pretty well," Avery said. "Seriously though," he continued, "all your hard work is beginning to pay off." Avery ran his hand across Blaze's shoulder. "Look how much her muscle tone has improved. And look at the shine on her coat. She's a different horse from the sad, skittish thing I dropped off here a few months back. You've done a fantastic job."

Issie blushed. She wasn't used to such praise from Avery. He was usually so tough on his riders that it meant a lot to her. But before she had time to feel too proud he was off again. "Still an hour left, people. Let's get them over some cross-country jumps. All right then, who's first? How about you, Ben?"

"Oh, no," Ben groaned. "Why do I have to go first? Max is totally hopeless today." He trotted off to warm up over a practice fence, while Dan trotted over to sit next to Issie and wait for his turn.

"Avery is right, you know," Dan said. "You and Blaze have come a long way."

"Thanks." Issie felt her cheeks flush pink for the second time.

"I suppose you're too busy training for the one-day event to take time out and go to Summer in the Park this weekend?" Dan asked.

Issie's heartbeat quickened. Was Dan asking her out on a date?

Summer in the Park was a series of gigs that local bands put on every year at Chevalier Point Park. Her mum had always said she was too young to go, but this year maybe she'd be allowed…

"Because if you are going," Dan continued, "we could always meet you there. Natasha and me are getting a whole group together. You should come along."

Natasha? Issie couldn't believe it. Suddenly Dan's invitation sounded less like a date and more like her tagging along while he hung out with Natasha.

"I didn't know you knew Natasha…" Issie was trying to sound casual, trying to keep the hurt out of her voice.

"She's in my class at school," Dan said, "and my mum knows her mum so we kind of made friends."

Dan was a year ahead of Issie, and didn't go to Chevalier Point High. He went to Kingswood, a school on the other side of town.

"We met at pony club the other day," Dan continued. "She told me she liked Smoothy, this really cool band who are playing this Sunday, so I said I'd take her along."

Issie couldn't believe it. How could Dan like Natasha? OK, she was sort of pretty in a boring girly blonde sort of way, but she was also stuck up and rude and mean-tempered. She couldn't believe Dan would fall for all that flirting Natasha did. It was so shallow and obvious.

"Typical! Boys are so, so… stupid!" Issie huffed under her breath.

"What's that?" Dan said.

"Umm, I said, I don't think I can make it. Sorry. I'm going to be really busy with Blaze this weekend. We still have a lot of work to do."

"Your turn Dan!" Avery shouted out. Ben had just completed his round and it must have gone well because he looked pleased with himself, riding back towards them wearing a grin from ear to ear.

"Dan, come on!" Avery yelled again.

"Ohmygod!" Dan groaned. "I was so busy talking, I haven't even warmed Kismit up yet."

He gathered up the reins and trotted off towards Avery, leaving Issie sitting by herself in the worst mood she had been in for weeks.

Issie was still in a sulk two days later, when she met up with Kate and Stella down at the River Paddock: "So then he tells me that he's going to Summer In The Park with Natasha!" Issie whined. "I don't know why he even asked me to come along at all!"

Kate and Stella both shook their heads in amazement as they listened to Issie's story of the whole stupid misunderstanding and how she thought Dan was asking her out when in fact he was going to the gig with Natasha.

"I can't believe he really likes her," Stella said. "That Natasha is just so pushy. I bet she's behind this."

"Well, it doesn't matter anyway," Issie said icily. "I've got too much to do getting Blaze ready for the one-day event to worry about a dumb concert."

Stella gave Kate a knowing glance. The two friends could tell Issie was really upset about Dan and Natasha, but she obviously didn't want to talk about it. The best thing to do was go for a good gallop and let the wind whip through her hair and blow the whole thing away.

For the past six weeks the girls had been riding to a strict training schedule that Avery had prepared for them in preparation for the one-day event. On Mondays and Wednesdays they practised their dressage tests. On Thursday and Sunday they practised jumps – showjumping and cross-country. And on Tuesdays, Fridays and Saturdays they did "interval training", trotting and cantering back and forth around the paddock until they were exhausted and the horses were wet with sweat. It was dull work and hard on a rider's bottom too. But today, instead of riding endlessly around the paddock, the three girls were taking the horses out for some road work, riding all the way to Winterflood Farm.

Winterflood Farm sat on a jut of green land right at the edge of Chevalier Point where the river met the sea. It wasn't a big farm, just ten acres divided into neat square paddocks fenced with posts and rails. A slender, tree-lined driveway ran down the middle of the fields leading to a gravel courtyard, which joined a stable complex to a small wooden cottage. The stables had been deserted for years until Tom Avery took over the farm. Now he kept his three young sport horses that he was training in the stables – although most of the time they grazed outdoors in the paddocks that surrounded the farm.

The girls would be able to ride across pasture land most of the way – the hunt club had a special route to Winterflood Farm that was open to all local riders.

"But we'll have to stick to a trot along the grass verges on the roadside until we get down to the bend in the river," Stella explained. "Then we'll be able to go cross-country so that we can get some good galloping practice in."

Issie felt a tingle of nerves. She had never galloped Blaze in the open countryside before, and after that ride in The Pines she was a little nervous about the hotheaded Arab bolting again.

"Are we ready to go?" Kate was dead keen to get Toby out on the open roads and start riding. So keen that the pair of them were pacing impatiently at the gate.

"Let's do it!" Issie clucked Blaze into a trot, but instead of rising up and down in her stirrups she stood up in them and practised her two-point cross-country position, balancing easily in midair with space to spare between her and the saddle.

Blaze jogged along, letting out snuffly snorts of excitement as if she knew they were leaving the paddock and going somewhere new.

"Remember to keep to single file near the roads," Stella shouted out. "I'll go up front with Coco since she's not likely to charge off. Issie, you can go in the middle with Blaze and Toby can bring up the rear."

The three of them set off at a brisk trot. A bit too brisk for Issie's liking – Blaze's trot was still bouncy enough to throw her about in the saddle, and she couldn't wait to reach open land so they could canter.

By the time they'd reached the open fields of the hunt-club land, the horses were in a sweat from the trot work. Tiny Coco was flecked with white froth on her neck and had green foam oozing out of her mouth from working the bit.

"Everyone ready to canter?" Stella yelled back over her shoulder. Issie and Kate both gave a silent nod and the three of them loosened the reins and let Coco, Toby and Blaze have their heads.

Issie looked down at the ground and watched as it became a blur of green and brown as Blaze cantered on. The chestnut mare was fast, Issie knew that much already. But it seemed that with each week, as her fitness improved, her speed increased.

"Steady, girl, easy now," Issie breathed to her horse, but the wind pushed her words back down her throat. Blaze had opened up and had started to gallop. She was wild with the thrill of running, and even with a firm hand on the reins Issie knew it would be hard to stop her now.

This time, though, instead of trying to hold the mare back, she gave Blaze her head and sat high in the saddle. *Let her run*, Issie thought. *Let's see what this horse can do.*

To the left of her, Kate was on Toby, urging

the long-limbed Thoroughbred on. Toby was an ex-racehorse, and yet, even at full gallop, Blaze could match him stride for stride. As the two horses ran on, Blaze's stride lengthened until she began to edge ahead of the big bay. By the time they reached the road leading to Winterflood Farm Blaze was ahead by a length. The mare's chestnut neck glistened with sweat and her breath was coming hard and raspy with the effort of the run.

"Easy, girl, slow down now." Issie tightened her grip on the reins and Blaze responded to the pressure, slowing her pace. Kate pulled Toby up next to her and the two girls and their horses came to a stop next to the farm gate to catch their breath.

"That was amazing!" Kate panted. "Toby was really stretching out back there and Blaze still beat him! I had no idea she was so fast!"

"Neither did I!" Issie said. She reached down and gave the mare a solid pat on her sweaty neck.

The sound of pounding hooves behind them made the two girls turn around. Stella and Coco were bearing down on them as fast as they could canter

"Thank God I've finally caught up with you two!"

Stella pulled Coco up to a halt. "I've been trying to get your attention ever since we started cantering." Stella looked concerned.

"Have you noticed it? Over there. That white van? Careful, don't let them see you looking!" Stella tried to gesture over her shoulder without actually turning around. Behind her a white van was parked on the grass verge that led to the hunt-club fields.

"Yeah, what about it?" Kate snapped. She was distracted, still having trouble hanging on to Toby as the Thoroughbred stomped about, all overexcited from his run.

"I'm sure it's the same one we saw the other day at the River Paddock," Stella whispered. "I know it sounds stupid, but I think it's following us."

"You know, they're parked miles away, Stella, they can't hear you, you don't need to whisper," Kate groaned.

"Look, I'm serious!" Stella insisted. "They've been driving along watching us. I'm sure of it. It's really creeping me out. I think we should turn around and go home."

"Nonsense!" Kate was in no mood for this now.

"You and your stories, Stella! I'm going over there to ask them what they want."

Without any more discussion on the matter she wheeled Toby around and cantered the big bay off towards the parked van.

In the distance the figures of two men suddenly sprang into motion. The driver, a short stocky type with a thick black bushy beard, jumped behind the wheel of the van while the other man, much skinnier and taller than the driver, ran around the van, quickly leaping into the passenger seat. The engine revved and, by the time Kate reached the grass verge, the van was gone.

"You were right," Kate had to admit as she trotted back to join the group. "They must have been watching us. At least they tore off in an awful hurry for some reason. This is creepy."

"I'll tell you what else is weird," Stella said. "You know how the spare paddock keys went missing the other day? Well I found them again! They were back on the hook in the shed as if they were there all along!" Stella narrowed her eyes. "I bet it's got something to do with those guys in the van."

Kate shook her head and sighed at Stella's latest revelation. "Oh, for heaven's sake, Stella, now you've got me falling for your crazy mystery stories! Those keys probably just got lost under that big mess of horse blankets you were chucking around."

"No, they didn't!" Stella was red-faced. "I looked everywhere for them! Someone took them and then they must have put them back again!"

"Anyway," Kate wheeled her horse around impatiently, "let's head for home." She looked across at Issie. "But no galloping this time, eh? I'm too exhausted. Let's just trot the rest of the way."

Issie nodded in agreement. But she wasn't really listening to Kate. She was looking up the road where the white van had disappeared. Stella was right. It was the same van they had seen parked down by the paddock the other day. And now the question was beginning to puzzle her. Just who were they following? And why?

CHAPTER 12

The dream started as it always did – with the sound of hoofbeats. Issie stared into the pitch-blackness, the thunder of hooves seemed to be surrounding her. This time, though, the grey horse didn't appear from the dark. Instead, the hoofbeats stopped and she could hear a soft whinny, calling to her, calling her out of sleep.

Issie woke with a start. Her dreams about Mystic had always seemed vivid, but never as real as this. She could have sworn she heard the neigh of a horse outside her bedroom window. She held her breath – there it was again! Only she was awake now, and still she heard it!

Issie crept up to the window as if she were stepping on broken glass, slowly, carefully. Through the lace of the curtain she could make out a shape moving on the lawn. She pulled the curtain back and peered out into the dark. It looked like a horse all right, but it was impossible to see properly. She would have to get dressed and go outside.

Quickly pulling on an old pair of jeans, a polar fleece and boots she ran for the back door that led to the lawn. Her mind was racing. How could a horse end up in her garden? She had an idea, but it was silly, impossible. She opened the back door and stepped out into the yard.

At first, she thought the horse must have vanished. In the dark it seemed like the green expanse of the lawn was empty. But then, in the corner of the garden underneath some tall birch trees she saw him. A dapple-grey, she could tell that much, even at this distance. But she needed to get closer. Silently she took one step, then another and then another, edging her way towards the horse. When she was a few metres away the little grey let out a low nicker, and stepped forward out from under the trees to meet her.

Tears filled Issie's eyes as she buried her head in the grey mane. It was Mystic. And he felt real and warm to her touch, not like a ghost horse, but like her own pony. She could even smell his sweet horsy smell as she kept her head pressed hard against his neck and tried to stop the tears from coming.

"Easy, boy, easy, Mystic," Issie cooed gently to him.

But Mystic would not stand still. He pulled away from her, shaking his head to free her hands from the tangle of his mane, and began to paw the ground in a frantic state. Then he let out a wild snort and wheeled about, racing all the way to the far end of the garden where the gate led to the street, then galloping back to stand in front of Issie. Again and again he repeated his frenzied run, charging up and down the lawn.

As Issie watched him gallop once more for the gate, she finally realised what Mystic was trying to tell her. He wanted her to ride him. Each time he ran down to the far end of the garden, Mystic came to a halt right in front of the five-barred gate that led to the street. Now Issie could see that the gate was the perfect height for her to climb up and mount the grey horse.

As he headed back down the lawn for the fourth

time, Issie ran after him. This time, when Mystic reached the gate he paused and waited for her to catch up to him. Then he stood still, snorting and quivering with anticipation as she clambered quickly up the gate rails and, hesitating just for a moment, threw herself lightly on to his back.

If this is a dream, Issie decided, *I must surely wake up now*. Instead she felt the sleek coat of her horse warm underneath her, and the ropey fibres of horsehair between her fingers as she buried her hands in Mystic's mane. The little grey leapt forward as he felt her weight on his back but Issie quickly calmed him, making him stand still so she could lean over to unlock the latch on the gate.

There was a slice of moon in the sky that provided just enough light so that Issie could make out the blurry outline of a horse beneath her. In the moonlight, Mystic's dappled coat seemed to melt into the night. It was almost as if she was riding a vapour, a wisp of grey smoke.

For a moment she wondered again whether she was dreaming. Then the clatter of hooves on tarmac jarred her back to reality as Mystic stepped through the gate and out on to the road. Now the streetlights were there to illuminate their path and Issie could clearly see her horse's grey ears pricked forward in front of her, swivelling occasionally to listen to the sound of her voice.

Issie clucked Mystic gently on, and without a bridle to steer with, she used her legs to guide the horse to the grass verge on the side of the road. With the soft grass underfoot she let the little grey break into a canter and felt a thrill tingle through her. She had forgotten how wonderful it was to ride this horse. The weeks of riding Blaze without a saddle had paid off, and Mystic's paces were so smooth and gentle, Issie felt as if she were riding a rocking horse. The summer breeze whipped her hair across her face. Blinded for a moment, she let her hands slip through Mystic's mane and had to scramble to grab another handful of horse hair.

"Even if this is a dream, I'd better hang on," she reminded herself. She realised now that there was no use steering. Mystic seemed to know where he was going. Instead of trying to guide the grey pony, Issie let him take her along for the ride.

The cold nip of the evening air made her eyes stream

tears, and the chill of the wind in her face froze a rosy pink glow on her cheeks. "Just hold tight," she told herself out loud. And at that moment she realised just what a strange picture the pair of them must make. A young girl, her black hair caught in the wind, her pyjamas sticking out from underneath the polar fleece jumper, riding bareback without a bridle in the middle of the night on a grey ghost, a horse whose dappled coat was hardly visible against the trees in the moonlight. No one would believe this. She didn't know whether to believe it herself. All she could do was hang on.

Away from the streetlights now, in the darkness, it was impossible to tell where they were. Now and then she would pass a house with the porch lights on and she'd be able to make out a familiar shadow or a street sign, but she was far too busy trying to stay on Mystic's back to look too hard at anything else around her. So at first, when Mystic came to a halt, she felt completely confused, directionless. Then she heard the sound of the river flowing fast and strong beside them and could make out the shapes of horses grazing in the field in front of them.

Of course! They were here, at the River Paddock.

But why? Why had Mystic brought her here tonight?

She was about to dismount and stretch her legs, try to figure out what was going on, when she heard the sound of a car engine cruising up the street behind her. Car headlights caught her in their beam, momentarily blinding her.

The drivers of the car couldn't have seen her because they kept driving straight past her towards the paddock gate. As they drove past, Issie's eyes adjusted back to the darkness. And then she saw who it was. Not a car at all, but a white van. The white van. The same one that had been parked outside the paddock watching them. The same one that had followed them on the ride to Winterflood Farm. The bearded man and the skinny one were sitting in the van just like before. But this time they were towing a red horse float behind them.

The van stopped and one of the men jumped out to open the gate to the horse paddock. Issie's mind was racing now. What were these men doing here? None of the horses that grazed at the River Paddock belonged to them. Besides, why would they come here in the middle of the night? What did they want?

On the other side of the van the door opened and a man stepped out. Then Issie saw he was holding a halter in his hand and she realised: they were here to steal a horse.

All this time, Mystic had been quiet underneath Issie, his dapple-grey coat was the perfect camouflage in this darkness amongst the willow trees by the river. There was no way the men could see them. But they might hear them. In the still of the night, Mystic gave a gentle nicker and the sound carried across the paddocks.

"What was that?" the big, bearded one barked out.

"What?" the other shouted back.

"That noise. It sounded like a horse."

"Well, of course it did, you idiot. We're at a horse paddock, aren't we? It's full of horses. Now stop mucking about, throw over those keys to the gate and then give me a hand. Remember, we're looking for a chestnut with four white socks. She shouldn't be hard to find – she's the only chestnut in the herd."

Issie felt her heart stop. A chestnut with four white socks? They could only mean Blaze. They were here to steal her horse! This was a nightmare. She had to

151

do something. But what? She could try to get to Blaze before they did, but in the dark there was no guarantee that she would find her horse first. And even if she caught Blaze, what then? There were two of them and their van was blocking the only exit in the paddock, making escape impossible. No, she had to stop these men. And for that she would need some help.

"Come on, boy, we've got to go," she spoke gently under her breath to Mystic, turning the little grey away from the paddock and back towards the Point. Winterflood Farm was ten minutes away at a fast gallop. If she could just find it in the darkness. And if she could only make it in time. She had to make it in time.

For the first minute, Issie had to force herself to keep calm and walk on. She was dying to get moving but she didn't want the men to hear the sound of Mystic's hooves pounding on the soft grass.

As soon as she knew she was safely out of range, Issie urged Mystic on into a canter, then a gallop. In the dark she knew it was risky. Mystic's night vision couldn't be much better than her own. There was always the chance that the grey pony might lose his footing or injure himself by getting a leg caught in a rabbit hole. But she had ridden this way before, just the other day on Blaze, and she knew it well enough.

Then there was the chance that at full gallop she might lose her balance, fall to the ground. Riding at this speed bareback was foolhardy at best. Issie knew that. But she also knew she had no choice.

If the wind had whipped her hair before, now it lashed it across her face with the sting of a birch branch. But she couldn't free her hands to wipe the strands away, she was too busy hanging on, clenching with her fingers so that Mystic's mane cut into the flesh of her hands. Her legs gripped firmly around the horse's belly, and she could feel herself sliding on Mystic's back as the grey pony became slick with sweat.

When she had ridden this same path on Blaze it had been daylight and she had the luxury of a saddle. Now, in the pitch black with nothing but her skill to keep her on Mystic's back, she was riding as if her life depended on it. *Now I know*, Issie realised. *Now I know what it's like to really ride a spirited horse.*

Despite the speed of Mystic's gallop, the ride from the River Paddock to Avery's house seemed to Issie like it took an entire lifetime. Then finally she heard the clatter of gravel under Mystic's hooves and they rode into the driveway of Winterflood farm.

Mystic pulled to a halt, but before he even had a chance to stop, Issie was vaulting lightly to the ground and running on her own. Running for Avery's front door.

She pressed the buzzer. Nothing. She pressed it again, hammering on the door too this time until her fists were sore. A light went on and then another, and then the door opened and the bleary-eyed face of Avery was staring at her full of amazement.

Ohmygod! Issie suddenly thought. *What if he sees Mystic?* But when she glanced back over her shoulder at the gravel courtyard the little grey was nowhere to be seen.

"Issie! It's three in the morning, girl! What the hell are you doing here?"

A thousand explanations seemed to choke themselves up in Issie's throat. She realised she had no time for words.

"Please, Tom, please. No time for that. Grab your coat and your car keys and let's go. Blaze is in danger."

CHAPTER 13

Avery drove the Range Rover at top speed back towards the River Paddock while Issie peered out into the darkness that surrounded them, keeping an eye out in case the white van was already making its getaway with the stolen horse onboard.

"We're almost there, Issie," Avery said, his eyes focused straight ahead, concentrating on the road in front of them. "So you'd better start explaining yourself now. What on earth is going on here?"

Issie quickly unfolded as much of the story as she could. She told Avery about the two men in the white van that had been following them, and how she arrived at the paddock tonight to find the same two men looking for Blaze and overheard their plans to steal her horse.

"When I left to find you they had grabbed a halter and a torch out of the van and they were hunting for her," she explained. "A chestnut with four white socks they said, and Blaze is the only chestnut that grazes at the River Paddock…"

"Wait a minute. What were you doing down at the paddock in the middle of the night all by yourself?" Avery asked.

"Ummm…" Issie faltered, "I was worried about Blaze, I guess. You know, because she's been so sick and with the event coming up. The weather had got so cold and I'd forgotten to put her cover on. I rode down to check on her on my bike and that's when I saw them."

Thankfully, it seemed that Avery was satisfied with this explanation.

He nodded his head thoughtfully, his mouth set in a grim line. Then he spoke.

"The question is, Issie, what are we going to do when we get there? There's just two of us, so I don't know how much use we'll be against two burly chaps.

Listen, you'd better hunt around in my glovebox there for my mobile. When we get to the paddock I'll go off and see if I can find these men and make sure they haven't hurt Blaze. Meanwhile you stay back at the car, and if you haven't heard back from me in about five minutes, give the police a call. Tell them what's going on as best you can and tell them to get down here straight away, that there's a theft in progress. Can you do that?"

Issie nodded. But she was worried. "Can't I come with you, Tom? There are two of them after all. You're going to need my help."

"It's too dangerous, Issie. You did the right thing coming to get me. Now do what I tell you and stay in the car."

They weren't far away from the paddock when Avery turned off the headlights on the Range Rover. "If they don't see us coming it will give us the element of surprise," he explained to Issie.

"That is if they're still there..." Avery squinted into the dark. "...I don't see anything in the paddock. Maybe they've already got Blaze loaded on and taken off..."

Issie's stomach churned as she peered desperately out into the gloom. There it was! The glow of the tail lights of a horse float. They hadn't gone. They were still there!

"Tom, over there!" she whispered.

"I see it," Avery confirmed. And with that, he switched off the Range Rover engine and let the car coast down the hill towards the paddock.

"Element of surprise again." He smiled at Issie. "We don't want them to hear us coming either, do we?"

The Range Rover coasted silently to the side of the road and Avery quietly unlatched his door and jumped out. "Change of plan," he said. "Call the police now, Issie. There's a chance we can catch these guys in the act. I'm going to take a snoop around and see what's going on. Now, remember, after you call the cops, you stay here in the car. I don't want you getting yourself into trouble." Avery gave her a reassuring smile and closed the car door.

Under the shadows of the willow trees Issie could just make him out now, hunched low to the ground, running towards the back of the tack room.

Issie picked up Avery's mobile and dialled the

police. Her heart was racing as she heard the dialling tone on the phone. The phone rang once, rang twice, rang a third time... and then stopped.

"Hello? Hello?" Issie's voice was wobbly with nerves. Why had the phone stopped ringing? Why wasn't anyone answering? She lifted the mobile up so she could see its digital face more closely. There in the right-hand corner a red light was flashing steadily on and off. She knew what it meant. Dead battery.

"Not now! It can't be!" Issie stared at the red light in disbelief. The mobile let out a low beep, a sign that the battery was about to die completely. *About to die*, Issie thought. *But it's not dead just yet. Maybe it still has enough power left to make one last call. Even if I don't get through to the police maybe somehow they can trace my signal or something.*

Issie didn't know much about how mobile phones worked. All she knew was that she had to try something. She dialled the police number again and hung on as the phone rang once, rang twice.

"Hello?" said a voice at the other end of the line. "Which service do you require – police, ambulance or fire?"

"Listen," Issie hissed, "I don't have much time. My phone is going dead. I need the police. This is Issie Brown. I'm down at the River Paddock near Waterstone Street and we need help…"

There was a dull buzz in her ear as once again the line cut out. Issie looked at the blinking red light. It was still flashing, so there must still be some juice left in the phone. Should she try again? She dialled the number once more. This time there was a dialling tone, the sound of a phone ringing and then nothing. Even the red light had stopped flashing now. There was nothing more that she could do. The battery was well and truly dead. Had the police got her message? There was no way of knowing.

Out there in the darkness, Avery was expecting help to arrive at any moment. He didn't know that the police might not be coming at all. She had to do something.

In the quiet night air the sound of the Range Rover door creaking open was almost deafening to her. She left the door hanging open, too afraid of the noise that shutting it might make, and crept forward from the car, staying low to the ground, sticking to the belt of trees that provided shadow cover.

Instead of climbing over the gate to get into the paddock, she slunk around behind the tack room and carefully, slowly, climbed over the wire paddock fence, using the wooden fence batons to balance herself. She landed lightly on the other side of the fence and there was a twang as a wire snapped back after being stretched by her foot during the climb.

"What was that?" she heard a voice say in the darkness, not more than ten metres away from her.

"What was what?" Another voice was talking now. "Probably just a possum. Don't worry about that, come over here. I finally caught that damn horse. Let's get her on to the float."

The field was suddenly lit up as the headlights of the white van were turned on, and Issie could see the two men clearly. One of them, the one with the beard, was leading a horse. Her horse!

Into the shining white beams of the headlights now stepped Blaze. Even from this far away Issie could see the whites of her eyes showing with fear. Her ears, normally pricked forward with excitement, were flat back against her head. As the man led her up to the ramp of the horse float she jerked back violently on the lead rope, trying desperately to back away.

"Stand still, you pig!" The man yanked the rope furiously, startling Blaze even further. "Stand still or I'll take the stick to you!"

He bent down to the side of the horse float, and when he stood up again Issie could see that he held a length of thick black rubber pipe in his hand. As he turned Blaze around to face the ramp of the float once more he lifted the rubber pipe in the air and brought it down hard and fast on the mare's flank.

Blaze let out a frightened squeal and jumped forward, not up the ramp of the horse float as the man had hoped, but out to the side of it. As she landed, her right hind leg caught on the edge of the ramp, grazing against it, and when she turned to face the ramp again Issie could see that she was bleeding. A steady trickle of dark red ran down her white hind sock.

"Give us a hand with this beast!" the fat, bearded

man yelled to his mate who was sitting in the front cab of the white van waiting to drive off.

"Can't you sort it out yourself?" the skinny one whined as he came around the back of the horse float to help.

"Stand there!" the bearded man instructed, pointing to the side of the horse-float ramp. "That way, she won't be able to escape to one side; she'll have no choice but to go on the float."

He turned Blaze again. This time as he went to lead her back towards the float, the chestnut mare reared up, pulling the lead rope almost out of his grip.

"That's it!" the man screamed with fury. "You're going on this float right now, or you're going to get the beating you deserve." He circled Blaze one more time, then, driving her towards the float, he lifted up the black length of pipe and brought it crashing down on her rump.

The final blow was too much for Issie to bear. She started to run forward, opened her mouth to shout out at the two men, to scream at them and make them stop hurting her horse. But before she could get a word out a hand covered her face from behind, and she felt the crushing weight of someone on top of her tackling her to the ground.

Issie tried to scream, but no sound could come out: her voice was stifled by the hand across her face.

"Shhh, shhh. It's OK. It's me," Avery growled in her ear. "Listen. I know you want to help Blaze, but this isn't the way. Stay where you are, stay quiet and trust me. Can you do that?"

Issie nodded mutely and Avery slowly removed his hand from her mouth. Together, the pair of them stayed on their bellies, lying flat on the ground and watched as Blaze, finally tired of the fight, placed one hoof after the other on to the ramp of the horse float and walked on board.

"Got her!" the bearded one said gleefully as he lifted up the tailgate behind her and closed the ramp, bolting Blaze in.

"Let's roll," he said to his friend, and the two men clambered back into the cab of the white van, ready to set off with their prize.

"Avery! We can't let them get away with this. We've got to stop them now!" Issie was almost in tears. The police hadn't arrived and these men had all but got away. They had to do something. She looked across at Avery who, strangely, had a sly smile on his face.

"Don't worry," he said, "they're not going far."

A minute passed, then another and another and still the two men in the white van didn't move. Then a door opened and Issie could hear the bearded man shouting, "The keys! The keys! How could you lose our keys? Well, come on, they've got to be here somewhere. Start looking!"

Issie looked at Avery in disbelief. "Tom, you didn't…"

Avery grinned and produced a set of shining silver car keys from his pocket. "I nicked them out of the ignition while the thin chap was helping to load Blaze into the float," he smirked. "They won't be getting far without these. Now all we have to do is wait for the police to turn up and…"

"Oh, Tom," Issie sighed, "that's the problem. I'm not sure that…"

Issie was about to explain the mobile drama when there was a sudden blare of a siren behind them and a flash of blue and red light. Two police cars had pulled up, blocking the exit at the paddock gate.

"The police!" Issie yelled. "They did get my message. They've come." Before Avery could say anything she was up off the ground and sprinting towards the police car.

With a sense of total relief, Issie watched as the rear door of the police car opened. She was about to blurt out the whole situation, explain to the police that they had to arrest these horse thieves who were trying to take her Blaze away. But as the figure emerged from the car, she found herself lost for words.

The person that stepped out of the police car wasn't a uniformed officer at all. It was her mother.

CHAPTER 14

It was five a.m. by the time they all arrived back at Avery's farm house. Mrs Brown headed straight for the kitchen. "I think we could all do with a nice hot mug of tea," she said, "and once I've sorted that out, Isadora, you've got some explaining to do."

Issie sighed and collapsed on to Avery's living room sofa. At first, when she had seen her mother emerge from the police car she had been relieved. But relief had quickly turned to terror when she realised that she still hadn't told her about Blaze. Her mum was right. She did have some explaining to do.

Mrs Brown reappeared from the kitchen now, with

three great steaming mugs of tea and some shortbread biscuits. "Is Tom back yet?" she asked her daughter.

"He shouldn't be much longer," Issie said. "He just had to give the police a few more details and then he was allowed to leave."

It already seemed as if they had been at the River Paddock for ever that evening. Once the police had arrived and the horse thieves had been taken away, Issie and Avery had been left with a young constable to answer some questions. Then they had been able to unlatch the horse float and let Blaze back out again.

The chestnut mare was naturally a little upset after her ordeal. Issie had taken her for a walk to calm her down and it was during the walk that she noticed Blaze was lame. She was favouring her right hind leg, the one that had been injured on the horse-float ramp. Issie had put an antiseptic on the cut, and wrapped the wound in a soft bandage to keep it clean. Then she had put antiseptic cream on the two deep gashes on Blaze's rump caused by the blows with the black rubber pipe. Finally, she had mixed Blaze up a special late-night supper – a mix of oats, hard feed and pony pellets with a wedge of hay on the side – and put her in the pen near the tack room so she couldn't do her leg any more damage overnight.

All of this time her mother had sat quietly in Avery's Range Rover waiting for her. But Issie knew that eventually her mum's patience would run out and it would be time to answer a few questions.

"Ah, excellent! Tea!" Avery stepped through the door, shedding his heavy jacket and boots in the corner of the kitchen. "Well done, Mrs B."

"I don't mind making the tea, Tom," Mrs Brown said, "as long as you don't mind explaining what you and my daughter were doing at that horse paddock in the middle of the night."

"Well," Avery began, "I've been talking to the police and it turns out that those two chaps they've caught are in fact Blaze's owners. That is, the ones that were mistreating her when the horse protection society found her. They must have seen Issie out riding on her and realised it was their horse and tried to steal her back again. Of course they've got no legal right to her. A complaint has already been lodged against them for what they did to Blaze and by rights they'll never be allowed to own any horse ever again. Although I'm still not completely convinced that they ever really owned one in the first place," he added.

"Blaze's bloodlines seem to be Anglo-Arab and I wouldn't be surprised if she's worth a lot of money..." Avery mused "...a lot of money. In fact, she's such a valuable mare, I suspect those men had already stolen her from someone else before we found her and saved her. I got the police to check their records to see if there had been a report of a horse theft that fits Blaze's description, but there was nothing on file.

"Naturally I told the officer that we'll be pressing charges over this whole matter. Horse thieves are bad enough, but people who abuse their horses are even worse," Avery growled.

"I'm sorry," Mrs Brown looked puzzled, "I still don't understand. What does all this have to do with Isadora?"

"Well," Avery said, failing to notice Issie making frantic gestures at him, "Blaze is her horse of course! She's done a fantastic job nursing her back to health after we recovered her from those criminals."

"Is that true, Isadora?" Mrs Brown looked at her daughter.

"I was going to tell you, Mum, honest," Issie pleaded, "only you were still angry at me for getting my belly button pierced. And then after that the time never seemed quite right. And then after I'd left it for a while, I didn't know how to bring it up. I mean, what could I say? I've owned a horse for three months now without mentioning it to you?"

"What?" Avery sputtered. "You mean you never told your mother about Blaze? Mrs B! I'm so sorry. I never bothered to tell you myself because I assumed that Issie had asked you and it was all OK..."

"Of course you did, Tom. Don't worry. It's not your fault. You, on the other hand," she exclaimed, turning to Issie, "I can't believe you! What if something had happened to you while you were out riding? Horses are dangerous, Isadora. You don't just charge off by yourself to go riding without telling me!

"And speaking of charging off..." Mrs Brown looked suspicious. "How did you get here in the middle of the night anyway? And how did you know those men would choose tonight to try to steal the horse?"

A chill passed over Issie. Mystic! Where was he? She

had left him outside in the driveway just next to the stables when she came to find Avery. The horse must have trotted off across the courtyard into the shadows by the stable block as Issie ran for the front door. And she hadn't seen him since. Now, sitting here in a brightly-lit living room, sipping tea and talking to her mum, she knew how ridiculous it would sound if she told the truth. The truth. That her horse, the horse that was supposed to be dead, had come to her bedroom window and warned her of danger. That she had ridden him bareback in pitch blackness halfway across town to catch the thieves, and that she now had no idea where he was, that he had disappeared.

"I rode, umm… I rode my bike here," Issie replied weakly, looking down into her tea cup.

"In the middle of the night? All the way across town? Issie, you could have been hit by a car!" Mrs Brown let out an exasperated gasp. "Look, I'm too tired to even begin discussing this here and now. We'll get to the bottom of it all tomorrow. Right now I think we should be getting home to try and get some sleep before it starts getting light." She stood up and passed her half-finished tea back to Avery.

"Thanks for the tea, Tom. We'll come back in the morning to pick up Isadora's bike, and I'll talk to you then about what is to be done with this horse that you've given my daughter." She paused. "Not too early in the morning, though; I imagine we'll all want a bit of a sleep-in after this. It isn't every night I get a wake-up call from the police dragging me out of bed at three a.m. and hopefully," she turned and frowned at Isadora, "I won't be getting any more calls in future."

Thankfully, Mrs Brown seemed content to let the whole Blaze affair drop during the car ride home. And after the evening's excitement Issie was grateful to slink off to her bedroom. She found herself falling asleep the moment her head hit the pillow. But instead of sleeping in, she was up again just a couple of hours later as soon as the dawn light came flooding in her window. In the dark last night it had been hard to tell just how serious Blaze's injuries really were. And with the one-day event now just a few days away she had to find out whether her horse was still fit enough to compete.

Of course there was another reason for getting up early. Last night Issie had lied to her mum, telling her that she rode her bike around to Avery's house. She could hardly tell her mother the truth, that she had galloped there bareback on a ghost horse in the middle of the night. In fact, she didn't even know if she believed the truth herself.

No, in this case it was definitely better to tell a white lie. The problem was, Mrs Brown was expecting to go around to Avery's later this morning and pick up the bike. The very same bike that was already parked exactly where it had been all along – right here at home in the corner of the garage.

The solution, Issie decided, was to leave her mum a note saying that she was walking over to Avery's to pick the bike up by herself. Then, instead of going to Winterflood Farm, she would cycle straight down to the horse paddock, check on Blaze and cycle home again.

Issie was feeling smug about her plan as she walked down the stairs to the front door. Until she saw her mother nursing a cup of coffee and flicking through the paper at the kitchen table.

"Up already?" Mrs Brown spotted her daughter heading for the door. "I'll put on some toast for you and make you a cup of tea and then we can go and pick up your bike."

"Ummm, thanks, Mum." Issie sat down reluctantly. Her plan was already falling apart and she hadn't even left the house yet!

"Isadora," her mother began, "I know I should be mad at you for what happened last night. God knows I should be furious that you've been riding this horse all this time and not telling me about it! But..." she paused to pour hot water into the teapot, "I guess in a way I can understand it. After the way I reacted to your belly-button thingamy-gig it's no wonder you were too scared to tell me about Blaze."

She sat down now and faced her daughter.

"I'm not saying that you were right to tear off and get your body pierced without telling me. Or worse yet, get a horse and fail to mention it for months! But maybe if I hadn't overreacted about that ring in your tummy. Or maybe if your father was still here..." Mrs Brown took her daughter's hand. "Issie, I know that since your dad left things have been tough, but we're getting on OK, aren't we? I'm on your side, remember that. I want you to feel that you can tell me anything, honey, OK?"

Issie nodded. Anything. Yeah right. She was sure "anything" didn't include going for midnight gallops on ghost horses. Still, her mother had a point.

"I do, Mum. And I'm sorry." Issie held her breath. *Might as well ask now*, she thought. "If you're not mad at me does that mean I can keep Blaze?"

"Well, if you've really managed to do such great things with her the way Tom says you have, I don't see how we have any choice." Mrs Brown smiled. "She must be a beautiful horse if those men wanted her so badly they were willing to steal her."

"She's perfect!" Issie glowed. And she started to tell her mother about how difficult Blaze had been to begin with, and how she had won her trust, and how the pair of them had been training for the one-day event.

"It's this weekend, so I hope Blaze's leg will heal in time. That's why I want to go down to the horse paddock this morning and check on her," Issie explained.

"What about your bike?" Mrs Brown said. "We can pick it up from Tom's on the way to the paddock."

"No!" Issie squawked. "I mean, if you drop me at the paddock I'll walk up to Winterflood Farm after I'm finished with Blaze and then I can ride the bike home."

"Well, OK. If that's what you'd prefer," Mrs Brown agreed.

And so, that afternoon Issie found herself walking the long roads back home from the horse paddock to her house, pretending to return a bike that was already safely locked up where it had always been, in the garage at her house.

At least, she thought to herself as she trudged along, *at least Blaze's wound seems to be healing well.* In fact when she had checked on the chestnut mare she seemed to be in fine spirits and was hardly favouring her injured leg at all. The chances were she would be well enough to compete at the one-day event. But with just days left, and lameness ruining their chances of fitting in any more training sessions, the question remained – was Blaze ready to go out there and win?

CHAPTER 15

In front of the green canvas marquee a crowd was beginning to gather. The judges had posted the dressage scores on a large whiteboard on the side of the tent and the riders were jostling about, trying to see over one another's heads, to check out how well they had done.

Stella, who had already pushed her way to the front of the crowd, peered hard at the board. "Let's see," she said, "novice dressage tests, group three… now where are we…" Her eyes scanned the board and then suddenly she let out a whoop of delight. "Issie, Issie," she yelled, racing across the field towards the area where the horse trucks were parked.

Issie was busily bandaging Blaze's tendons in preparation for the cross-country when she heard Stella hollering out her name.

"Issie! You'll never believe it," Stella panted with exhaustion as she reached her friend. "I'm coming fourth out of the whole novice class. Fourth place in dressage – can you believe it?"

Before Issie had a chance to answer Stella was off again, "And that's not all. Guess what? You're coming second! Isn't that cool?"

"I don't believe it!" Issie was stunned. "Do you hear that, girl?" she said to Blaze, who was busy making short work of her breakfast hay net. "We're in second place."

After all they had been through in the past week, Issie was amazed to be here at all. Yesterday the vet had arrived at the River Paddock, given Blaze's hind leg a final checkup and pronounced her perfectly sound. And today, here they were – riding at their first one-day event.

This morning in the dressage ring Blaze and Issie had managed to put the past week behind them and performed a perfect test. Even so, Issie could scarcely have hoped for such a result. After all, there were nearly sixty riders here today competing in her class.

"Did you see who's coming first?" Issie asked the overexcited Stella.

"You're not going to believe this one either," Stella groaned. "It's Natasha. She's in first place on fifty-nine points. You're right behind her on sixty-one."

Issie was puzzled. "How come I'm behind her if I've got more points?"

"Man, you really are green at this game, aren't you?" Stella giggled. "The winning dressage rider is the one with the *lowest* score. You take each dressage score and you add the faults that the rider gets in the cross-country and then the faults from the showjumping, and the one with the lowest score at the end of it all is the winner.

"The dressage score is important," Stella continued, "but it's the cross-country that is crucial. You get twenty faults for every refusal and sixty faults if you fall off. It doesn't matter how good your dressage score is if you have to add sixty faults to it! The showjumping isn't so tough – it's just five faults for every rail.

"So," Stella grinned at her friend, "all you've got to do now is go clear on the cross-country and the showjumping and you're in the running for a ribbon."

"Yeah, right," Issie joked, "two clear rounds? That sounds really easy – not!"

"We'll see about that." Avery's voice behind her caught her off-guard. "Come on, girls. Tie your horses up and let's get a move on and walk the course."

Walking the cross-country course was a crucial part of the one-day event, and earlier that day Avery had offered to take Issie and Stella around the fences on foot, pointing out the different angles and approaches for the fences and the best way to handle each obstacle. However, she hadn't counted on the fact that Dan and Ben would be coming with them as well.

As Avery's students set off towards the first fence of the course, Dan slowed down so that he and Issie were walking together at the back of the group.

"Hey, Issie!" Dan seemed excited to see her. "I heard all about what happened with you and Blaze. Pretty freaky stuff, huh? It sounds like you and Avery were real heroes, catching those guys like that."

"Mmmm..." Issie tried to act casual. Inside, she

was dying to tell Dan all about how they saved Blaze from the horse thieves. But she was still in a huff with Dan over the whole Natasha thing so she felt obliged to give him the silent treatment instead.

"Are you OK, Issie?" Dan's cheery tone was beginning to slip a little. "I mean, I know you must have been pretty busy over the past week or so but I was kind of hoping you would come along to Summer in the Park with me."

"With you and Natasha, you mean!" Issie snapped and then realised what she had done. *Ohmygod*, she thought. *Now Dan will realise that I'm jealous of him and Natasha. This is so embarrassing...*

"Gather round, everyone, let's check out jump number one." Avery interrupted her thoughts as he drew their attention to the first fence, a rustic wooden rail that stood around eighty centimetres high and was strung with old car tyres.

"This is a simple fence, with a clean take-off and landing point," Avery briefed them. "What I want you to concentrate on here is getting a smooth stride happening. Your horse should already be in a steady cross-country gallop. I want you to check them a few strides out and bring them back to a strong canter, then pop over it and pick up the pace again. It shouldn't give you any trouble."

"Issie," Dan whispered in her ear as Avery kept talking, "Issie, I think you have the wrong idea about Natasha and me."

No use trying to act cool about this now, Issie thought to herself; Dan knew what she was thinking. "Well, if you mean that Natasha is your girlfriend, I think I've got the right idea," Issie muttered back.

"Girlfriend!" Dan squeaked. "No way! Issie, I only took Natasha to Summer in the Park because her mum asked my mum if I would take her along. I mean, they've only just moved to Chevalier Point and, well, I know Natasha can come across as really snobby, but I think maybe that's just because she's got no friends here and she's afraid of us because we're all so close and we all get on so well… Well," he added glumly, "at least I thought we did, but lately I'm not so sure. You won't even talk to me."

"Jump number two, quite a wide ditch, this one," Avery explained. "Your horse is likely to take off too soon and bunny hop across, so keep your legs on…"

But Issie wasn't listening. Her head was buzzing now. So Dan wasn't interested in Natasha after all!

"I'm sorry if I haven't been myself lately." Issie smiled at Dan, taking in his thick waves of blond hair and soft blue eyes. "I guess I've just been really worried about things – you know with Blaze nearly being stolen and everything. But yes, of course we're friends. And maybe you're right about Natasha," she added, "but I'm still not so sure. She seems pretty stuck-up to me."

With the misunderstanding cleared up, Issie and Dan walked the rest of the course in silence, concentrating on Avery's advice.

"Now this is truly a natural obstacle." Avery grinned as they neared the end of the course. Issie found herself standing at the edge of a deep gully with steep banks on either side. To enter the gully, riders had to jump over a large fallen tree, and then immediately after the tree the ground fell away steeply so that the horses literally slid down a muddy slope until they reached the bottom of the gulch, where another fence was constructed out of oil drums. The horses would have to leap over the drums before cantering back up the other side of the mud bank, taking the post-and-rails fence that sat at the top of the ridge.

"I'd like you to slow down to a trot coming into this one," Avery said. "The fallen tree is a quite a big spread, but the horses should be able to jump it at a trot, and approaching at a slow pace will give them enough time to realise that there's a steep bank behind the fence – so they don't spook at the last minute. Then, once you're over the tree, all you really need to do is hang on. The horses will be moving pretty fast down the muddy bank and they'll have no trouble with the oil drums. Then they'll power back up the other side and take the post and rails. They'll really be flying by them, so hang on."

It made Issie nervous to see that the ambulance van, which was always present at events like this one, had parked itself at the top of the gully next to the fallen tree. "They must be expecting some crashes here." She nudged Dan and pointed towards the white van. He nodded in agreement.

"After the hollow, the trick will be calming them down again and getting them back into stride to take the next fence," Avery explained as he approached the cotton reels.

The cotton reels were a row of huge wooden spools that looked like they might once have been part of a giant's sewing kit. Issie didn't know what they had really been used for, but she guessed they were from a construction yard or something. They were big – she knew that much. And the horses would have to jump clean over them.

"Finally, we have the bank," Avery said, turning his attention to the last fence, a high grassy mound that the horses had to jump up on to, then canter along for two strides before jumping a fence that dropped away dramatically to ground level.

"By now your horses will be dead tired," Avery continued, "so don't thrash them by racing for the finish flags. By all means, keep your speed up to try and avoid time faults, but don't exhaust your mounts. Remember, there's still the showjumping to come after this."

Back at the horse truck Issie took out Avery's prized flat-seat saddle and began to tack Blaze up in preparation for the cross-country. The mare knew that today was special somehow. The sight of the horse floats and trucks and the noise of the loud speaker had her keyed up and she danced as Issie tried to do up her girth.

"Easy, girl, you'll get the chance to show them how good you are any minute now," Issie whispered to her horse.

She swung herself into the saddle and was adjusting the competition number attached to her back protector when Stella rode over to see her.

"I was just down at the judges tent and it looks like Natasha has gone clear on the cross-country. No faults! Can you believe it? You'll have to get a clear round now if you want to keep up."

"Thanks heaps," Issie groaned, "that's just what I need, Stella – more pressure. I'm nervous enough as it is."

"Competitor number thirty-eight please, number thirty-eight." Issie looked down at the number on her chest. "That's me. Wish me luck," Issie said. But she was too nervous to hear Stella's reply.

"Are you ready? Lining up now… five, four, three, two, one… go!" The starter's gun sounded and Issie felt the chestnut mare leap out from underneath her and instantly break into a gallop, her long stride devouring the ground. She let Blaze run on until the first fence was in sight, then she eased her back, collecting her into a canter. Blaze gave an indignant snort and popped over the tyres as if they were barely there, moving swiftly back into a gallop again.

Riding crouched over her neck, Issie felt the rush of speed, the power of the horse beneath her. At the ditch, Issie was cautious again and slowed Blaze down, but the mare popped over it with ease.

The next fence was a three-barred gate stuffed with dried brush. Issie heard the thick rasp of the branches scraping against Blaze's bell boots as they breezed over it. She gave the mare her head and let her gallop on to the next part of the course.

As they tackled fence after fence without missing a stride Issie's confidence grew. Not only was Blaze's leg completely healed, the horse seemed to thrill at the chance to run. So much so that it was tempting to let her have her head as they approached the gully. Still, Issie remembered Avery's advice and pulled hard on the reins, easing Blaze back to a steady trot so that she had time to get a good look at the fence.

They were still a good few strides out from the jump when Blaze spooked. Issie lost a stirrup and was nearly thrown out of the saddle as her horse lurched suddenly to the left.

"Come on, girl, what's wrong?" Issie kicked her on, hauling on the right rein at the same time to get Blaze back on track. But it was no use. Blaze was in a state, highly-strung and confused, not listening to Issie's aids. The mare trotted up skittishly towards the jump, then spooked again at the last minute and came to a dead stop.

Issie couldn't believe it. A refusal would cost them twenty faults! Not only that, but now Blaze was standing there in front of the jump all wild-eyed and trembling with fear. What on earth was wrong with her?

As she tried to calm her horse, Issie's mind began

to race. Why was Blaze so terrified? It wasn't the fence, she was sure of that. Blaze had taken jumps just like this one before without any trouble. No, she decided. Something else had scared her horse – and it was still spooking her now. And if Issie didn't figure it out quickly her chances of winning the one-day event were doomed.

CHAPTER 16

As Blaze stood trembling in front of the fence, Issie looked up at the white ambulance van parked at the top of the ditch and suddenly everything clicked into place.

It was a white van. A van just like the one the men had used when they had tried to steal Blaze. Of course! It wasn't the fence that had spooked the horse but her fear of the white van that had made her refuse the jump.

Issie circled her horse away from the fallen tree now, talking softly to her, "It's OK, Blaze, no one's going to hurt you." She spoke calmly and gently.

Issie knew that normally when a horse is afraid of something the best thing to do is confront their fear. If she gave Blaze the chance to check the van out thoroughly, eventually she would no longer be afraid of it. But right now there was no time for that solution.

Instead, Issie turned to take the fence again, this time aiming her horse at a sharp angle, so that she was facing away from the van.

Approaching the jump on the diagonal wasn't easy, and it also meant taking Blaze down the slipperiest part of the slope, but Issie knew it was the only way.

With the white ambulance out of her line of sight, Blaze was a different horse. She leapt easily over the fallen tree and powered down the hill, over the oil drums and up and out the other side over the post and rails. "Good girl." Issie gave her a firm slap on her sweaty neck.

Blaze was back in good spirits, all memories of the white van were put behind her. Now there were only two fences to go.

At the cotton reels, she flew over the jump with almost half a metre to spare and it was all that Issie could do to slow her down in time to take the grassy bank.

Riding up the bank, Issie tried to remember to sit well back in the saddle, then lean back as Blaze leapt off into midair to land on the ground below.

And then they were racing, Issie leaning low over Blaze's neck and pushing her home through the finish flags.

"Oh, well done, girl, well done!" Issie was thrilled. Blaze's fright at the sight of the white van had cost them dearly. Twenty faults for a refusal. But they had been going so fast around the course they had no time penalties in spite of their delay at the gully. And with the showjumping still to come, maybe they stood a chance of a ribbon – if they could make it a clear round.

As the totals went up on the scoreboard for the cross-country Issie was amazed. It looked like hardly any of the other riders had managed a clear round either. Even with twenty faults, her chances of a ribbon looked good. In fact she was still in second place – only Natasha had gone clear on the cross-country to stay ahead of her. Poor Stella had had three refusals at the cotton reels and had retired on Coco. She was too depressed to come with Issie to check out the scores and was back at the horse truck giving Coco a good brush down before rugging her up. Her disastrous cross-country meant that she wouldn't be riding in the showjumping.

The first competitors for the showjumping phase were beginning to warm up now, and it wouldn't be long until they entered the ring. Issie looked across at the showjumps and saw Natasha leaning up against the rails, waiting to see how the other competitors tackled the course before she too began to warm up.

The sight of Natasha filled Issie with dread. She wanted to hide – to duck out of sight behind the horse floats and avoid her. But then she remembered what Dan had said about Natasha not being mean really, just lonely. So she decided to do the grown-up thing and go over and say hi.

"Hey there, Natasha." Issie smiled. "It looks like

you and Goldrush have been having a good day; you've got the top score so far."

Natasha turned around and gave Issie a snooty look. "I'm sorry? Do I know you?" she said vaguely, acting like she had never met Issie before. Her lips curled up in a wicked smile. "Oh yeeesss," she purred, giving Issie the once-over as if she were being asked to give her points out of ten for her appearance. "You're that girl from the pony club, aren't you? The one with the scruffy chestnut. What are you doing here?"

Issie couldn't believe it. Why was she even bothering with this snob? *Keep calm*, she told herself. *Remember, she's only trying to be mean because she feels insecure. Remember she's new in town and she has no friends.*

"I'm riding actually," Issie said, trying to keep her smile fixed to her face. "In fact, I'm coming second to you. We had a little problem on the cross-country. Blaze got spooked at the top of the gully and we had a refusal and got twenty faults."

"Mmmm?" said Natasha. She clearly couldn't be bothered talking to Issie at all and was looking away now to watch the next competitor enter the ring.

"Well, sounds like you need to get a decent horse, don't you? Or maybe some riding lessons."

And with that, she turned back to watch the showjumping, leaving Issie standing with her mouth hanging wide open.

"I mean, just because her mother buys her some flash horse doesn't make her such a great rider!" Issie fumed to Stella. The pair of them were back at the horse truck now and Issie was tacking up for the showjumping.

"A decent horse? And she called Blaze scruffy. Scruffy! She's got such a nerve! I should have told her that Blaze was actually part Arab and she's probably worth more than she paid for silly old Goldrush anyway. Oh, who cares! She doesn't even really like horses, you know. And no wonder she doesn't have any friends. I should never have listened to Dan. I don't know how he can even put up with her for a minute!"

"Issie, Issie calm down." Stella laughed. "It's nearly your turn for the showjumping. Shouldn't you be taking Blaze over a few practice jumps instead of worrying about Stuck-up Tucker?" Stella glanced across at the show ring. "Hey," she said to Issie, "wait a minute. It's Natasha's turn now."

"She hasn't knocked down four rails, has she?" Issie was sulking, refusing to look. "Because that's how many points she needs to lose before I'll beat her."

"Umm, no… but..." Stella said. "Oh, oh wait a minute. Ohmygod!"

"What? What is it? What's happening?" Issie had completely forgotten about her sulk and stopped what she was doing to join Stella.

In the showjumping ring, Natasha was far from her usual smug self. Goldrush had refused at the green gate twice now, and as she turned her a third time to face the fence, giving her a thwack across the rump with her crop, the palomino reared up, promptly dumping Natasha on the ground.

"You brute!" Natasha screamed, still hanging on to the reins with one hand and making a lunge across the ground to pick up the riding crop with the other.

Goldrush backed away from her, snorting with fear, but Natasha hung on to her and, with the crop in her fist, she raised her hand high above Goldrush's head and prepared to bring the whip down. "That's the last time you do that to me, you useless animal!" Natasha cried as she brought the whip down hard.

But before the riding crop could connect with its target, a large hand was wrapped around Natasha's arm, holding her back. "And that's the last time you hit a horse, young lady. You're disqualified," Tom Avery said. "Now come with me to the judges' tent. I'm sure they'd like to discuss this bad-tempered performance with you in person."

"Competitor number thirty-eight into the ring please," the announcer's voice came over the loud speaker. At the far end of the practice paddock Issie popped Blaze one last time over the practice jump and then cantered towards the gate.

With Natasha out of the competition, Issie was in the lead, but there was no room for even a single mistake. Knocking down just one rail would lose her five points and drop her back all the way to third place. Two rails would cost her ten points and she'd lose out on a ribbon entirely. No, it had to be a clear round or nothing.

At fence one it looked like it was going to be nothing! Forgetting Avery's constant advice to remember to ride at the first fence seriously, she approached the jump far too slow, not really concentrating on it, and Blaze almost baulked. Luckily the fence wasn't huge and the chestnut mare was so honest she took the jump anyway, leaping like a jack rabbit almost from a standstill, flinging Issie back in the saddle.

The fright at fence one woke Issie's ideas up. She collected Blaze up into a bouncy canter and rode hard at the second fence, clearing it perfectly. Then came a double with a bounce stride, and Issie had to check Blaze hard to slow her down so she wouldn't rush the fences.

With a clear round so far and only two fences to go, Issie was sick with nerves as they approached the green gate where Goldrush had been eliminated. The gate was the biggest fence on the course. There were two slender potted conifers standing on either side of it and the jump was so tall it was almost as big as the trees themselves. It had to be nearly one metre twenty,

Issie decided. It was almost the biggest fence she had ever faced.

"Still not as high as that gate between the River Paddocks though, eh, girl?" Issie murmured to Blaze. She tightened her grip on the reins, sat back hard in the saddle and pushed the chestnut mare on. Blaze flew over the jump, flicking her heels up beautifully so that she didn't even touch the poles. Then over the last fence and through the finish flags. A clear round.

"Oh, Issie, you did it!" Stella came racing up as Issie emerged from the ring. "Wasn't Blaze fantastic? Just the best!" Stella was bubbling with excitement. She took Blaze by the reins and led the mare back towards the truck as Issie walked alongside them, still feeling a little stunned by her own success.

"Well, well. Who would have thought that my groom would be such a star?" Issie turned around to see Dan smiling at her. "Seriously, Issie, congratulations. It was a brilliant bit of riding…" he said. He was about to say something more when Issie heard her name being shouted out across the field.

"Isadora! Isadora!" Issie's mum had her hands full

with a tea thermos, an umbrella and a blanket, most of which got dropped on the grass as she ran up to her daughter.

"Oh, well done, sweetheart!" she said, letting everything in her arms tumble to the ground now as she embraced Issie in a huge bear hug.

"And well done, Blaze!" Mrs Brown said, and she reached out a careful hand to give the mare a tender pat on the nose.

"Mum!" Issie was shocked. "I thought you didn't like horses?"

Mrs Brown looked her daughter in the eyes. "Oh, Issie, I still don't like horses. When I think of all the danger that you've been through over the past few months…" she sighed. "But I know that you love them," she turned to the little chestnut, "so I guess that means Blaze and I are going to have to be friends, aren't we, girl?"

She stepped forward to give the horse another nervous pat and Blaze, eagerly anticipating that she might be in for a treat, gave Mrs Brown a vigorous, snuffly nudge with her nose. Issie's mum jumped back with a shriek and everyone else burst out laughing.

"She just wants a carrot, Mrs B – I think she likes you!" Dan was smirking.

"Well," said Mrs Brown, smiling back now, "I guess after today's performance she deserves one. Now hurry up and get back on," she told her daughter. "You don't want to be late for the prize-giving, do you?"

Blaze was still wearing her winner's ribbon when Issie unloaded her from the horse truck back at the River Paddock later that evening. The deep red satin sash was knotted around her neck, with its gold fringing dangling down.

"You look like a proper Arab now, all dressed up with gold fringes," Issie teased the mare. But there was some truth in what she said. Blaze didn't even resemble the sickly pony that Issie had adopted three months ago. This was a horse in her prime and her fine bloodlines were finally in full evidence, from the high arch of her graceful neck to the soft dish of her face with its pure white blaze.

"You're so beautiful, I can hardly believe you're

mine," Issie whispered into Blaze's neck as she gave her a hug, undoing the sash at the same time and shoving it into the pocket of her riding jacket.

"Pretty exciting, eh? Winning your first one-day event?" Avery's voice behind her startled her.

"I guess so," Issie said, "but after all we've been through in the past few weeks I think I've had enough excitement. Mostly I'm just glad that Blaze is OK."

Avery ran his hand down the mare's hind leg. "That wound seems to be completely healed. You probably won't even be able to see the scar, Issie."

He looked back up at his star pupil.

"That night of the horse thieves, there's something I'm still puzzled about," Avery said. "I know you told your mother that you had cycled to my house. But I'm sure I didn't see your bike in my driveway. Besides, how did you know they were going to try to steal Blaze in the first place? Issie, do you want to explain to me what really happened that night?"

Issie smiled. "I've been going over and over it in my mind, and no, I can't explain it. At least not yet. I'm not even really sure I understand it myself."

Avery nodded, "Well, if you ever want someone

to talk to, give me a try. I bet you'll find me more understanding than you think."

After Avery had loaded off the other horses, he backed the truck out the gate and left Issie alone in the paddock with Blaze.

Even though she ached all over and was dying for a hot bath, Issie knew she had to take care of her horse before she could finally go home. In the tack room she scooped out four big handfuls of pony pellets and mixed in some oats and a little chaff. Then she grabbed Blaze's cover off a hook on the wall.

As the chestnut mare ate her dinner, Issie did up the cover straps and unbandaged Blaze's legs. Then when she'd finished the last of her food, Issie slipped the halter off her slender head and let her loose.

"Typical!" Issie grinned as Blaze trotted off, her nose trailing the ground, heading straight to the dustiest patch in the paddock to have a good roll. Dropping to her knees, Blaze gave a satisfied grunt, then a series of ecstatic groans as she rolled from one side to the other, getting herself covered in thick dirt in the process.

Standing up again, the mare shook herself and a cloud of dust rose off her cover. There were clumps of grass stuck in her mane.

"Oh, Blaze," Issie sighed, "it'll take me hours to groom that out!"

But Blaze wasn't listening. She had headed off down the paddock in a high-stepping trot, her head held erect. Issie watched as the mare let out a shrill whinny, looking for paddock mates. She was surprised when she heard another whinny in reply.

The whinny rang out across the paddock and then, at the far end of the field, down by the river, Issie saw him. A grey horse. Not a big horse, no more than fourteen hands probably. Light grey, with his dapples faded from old age. As he whinnied again, Blaze lifted her head and broke into a canter, running to him.

Issie watched in silence as the two horses began to run together. Over the past few weeks she had begun to think that maybe Mystic was her guardian angel. Now, as she saw her two horses together, Issie wondered: was it really her that Mystic had been looking after? After all, it was Blaze's life that he had saved. Was it possible that horses could have guardian angels of their own?

"Don't worry, Mystic," Issie called out to him, "I'll take good care of her."

She turned her back on the horses and threw Blaze's halter over the handlebars of her bicycle. It was getting dark and it was a long ride home.